PRAISE FOR JEN CALONITA'S FAIRY TALE REFORM SCHOOL SERIES

"Another winner from Jen Calonita. Charming fairy-tale fun."

> —Sarah Mlynowski, author of the *New York Times* bestselling Whatever After series on *Flunked*

"Fairy Tale Reform School is spell-binding and wickedly clever. Gilly is smart, spunky, and a hilarious narrator, and I cannot wait to read about her next adventure!"

> —Leslie Margolis, author of the Annabelle Unleashed novels and the Maggie Brooklyn mysteries on *Flunked*

"Fairy Tale Reform School is a fresh and funny take on the enchanted world. (And, who hasn't always wanted to know what happened to Cinderella's stepmother?)"

> —Julia DeVillers, author of the Trading Faces identical twin series and *Emma Emmets, Playground Matchmaker* on *Flunked*

"This clever novel and its smart, endearing cast of characters will have readers enchanted and eager for the implied sequel(s)."

"Gilly's plucky spirit and determination to oust the culprit will make *Flunked* a popular choice for tweens."

"There's much to amuse and entertain fans of classic tales with a twist."

"New readers will be caught up within the first few pages. Tweens who are fans of fractured fairy tales like the Whatever After series by Sarah Mlynowski will have no problem getting into this read."

"Gillian remains an appealing, vibrant character, whose first-person narrative, with humorous, dramatic, and self-reflective touches, makes for fast-paced, entertaining reading."

"Mermaids, fairies, trolls, and princesses abound in this creative mashup of the Grimms' most famous characters. This whimsical tale is a surprising mixture of fable, fantasy, and true coming-of-age novel."

—Kirkus Reviews on *Tricked*

"An entertaining and often humorous fantasy flight. Recommended for fans of Soman Chainani, Shannon Hale, and Shannon Messenger."

—School Library Journal on *Tricked*

"This fast-paced mashup of fairy tales successfully tackles real-life issues such as prejudice, gender-role conformity, and self-esteem."

—Kirkus Reviews on *Switched*

"This entertaining series will satiate readers for whom Disney's *Descendants* is a year or two out of reach."

—School Library Journal on *Switched*

ALSO BY JEN CALONITA

FAIRY TALE REFORM SCHOOL

Flunked

Charmed

Tricked

Switched

Wished

Cursed

ROYAL ACADEMY REBELS

Misfits

Outlaws

CURSED

FAIRY TALE REFORM SCHOOL

CURSED

JEN CALONITA

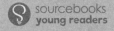
sourcebooks
young readers

Published by Sourcebooks Young Readers, an imprint of Sourcebooks Kids
P.O. Box 4410, Naperville, Illinois 60567-4410
(630) 961-3900
sourcebookskids.com

Library of Congress Cataloging-in-Publication Data

Names: Calonita, Jen author.
Title: Cursed / Jen Calonita.
Description: Naperville, IL : Sourcebooks Young Readers, [2020] | Series: Fairy Tale
    Reform School | Audience: Ages 10 and up.
Identifiers: LCCN 2019052809 | (hardcover)
Subjects: CYAC: Fairy tales--Fiction. | Characters in literature--Fiction.
    | Magic--Fiction. | Blessing and cursing--Fiction. | Heroes--Fiction. |
    Reformatories--Fiction. | Schools--Fiction.
Classification: LCC PZ7.C1364 Cur 2020 | DDC [Fic]--dc23
LC record available at https://lccn.loc.gov/2019052809

This product conforms to all applicable CPSC and CPSIA standards.
Source of Production: Worzalla, Stevens Point, Wisconsin, United States
Date of Production: March 2020
Run Number: 5017786

Printed and bound in the United States of America.
WOZ 10 9 8 7 6 5 4 3 2 1

For the newest member of the Calonita family, Massimo Campagna.

Once a villain, always a villain.

Happily Ever After Scrolls

Brought to you by FairyWeb—Enchantasia's Number One News Source!

Royal Court Clash at Enchantasia Village Meeting

by Coco Collette

Tensions were high at last night's emergency village meeting attended by Enchantasia's royal court. Reigning princesses Ella, Rapunzel, Snow, and the recently returned Sleeping Beauty, Rose, spoke to a large crowd about what is being done to protect citizens from the wrath of Rumpelstiltskin and recently returned Evil Fairy Alva. "Both the royal guard and the Dwarf Police Squad are spread out across the kingdom looking for signs of these villains," Rapunzel told the audience. "We are dedicated to protecting our people and preventing these villains from spreading fear throughout the land."

This *HEAS* reporter made waves when she mentioned an anonymous tip she received about the two villains. "I'm told they're trying to get the remaining ingredients they need to enact a curse on Enchantasia and alter the course of history," this reporter said.

A woman in the back row fainted. Another screamed, "Is it true? Is Enchantasia about to be cursed?"

"What ingredients do they still need?" interrupted another. "Why aren't you trying to stop them?"

"We cannot comment on the curse at this time," Rapunzel replied, to which the room erupted in both shouting and tears. Pattycake Bakersman even threw handfuls of flour at the royal court. He was quickly apprehended by Dwarf Police Chief Pete and taken away.

(In hindsight, perhaps this reporter should have questioned the royal court in private, but award-winning reporters like me never shy away from the tough questions.) Princess Ella tried to bring the room back to order. "Please trust that the royal court is not sitting idly by. Even as I speak, individuals with skills far superior to my own are working to keep these villains from cursing anyone. We must remain calm and stay vigilant."

"How?" said one individual. "We can't defend ourselves against a curse that rewinds time!"

"How do I protect my family?" shouted another.

"And who is protecting the students at Fairy Tale Reform School? Or Royal Academy now that Headmistress Olivina has gone missing?" asked a woman.

"Well…" Princess Ella looked at the rest of the royal court for guidance.

"Has Olivina joined the villainous ranks of Mr. Stiltskin and Alva?" asked a man holding a crying baby.

"We aren't sure, but—" Rapunzel was quickly interrupted.

"Fear not about Royal Academy!" Princess Rose stood to greet her public. "I will happily take up the headmistress title at the school until a new headmistress has been found." Villagers cheered.

"Uh, Princess Rose, I don't believe we've discussed that matter yet," Snow interjected.

"Are you saying I wouldn't be a good headmistress?" Rose countered.

"I'm saying you fell under a villain's spell once before, and running a royal school with a headmistress who has questionable allegiances might not be the best move," Snow replied. Many in the audience gasped.

"I am a beloved princess who deserves a second

chance!" Rose cried (like literally cried, which caused the Rose groupies in the back to stand up with their *Princess Rose Is Number 1* signs and cheer).

"May we please have some order?" Princess Ella begged to no avail.

Suddenly there was a gust of wind, and the room went dark. People screamed and hid under their chairs. When the torches relit, Headmistress Flora of Fairy Tale Reform School and Professor Harlow (a.k.a. the former Evil Queen) were standing in the center of the room.

"Silence!" Professor Harlow glared at the assembled villagers. "When the royal court tells you all to shush, you shush!"

The silence was so loud Princess Ella's mice friends could be heard squeaking in terror inside a wall.

"Finally! " Professor Harlow's purple cape swirled around her. "Now Flora has something to say."

"During times like these, we must pull together," Headmistress Flora implored. "Villains try to tear us apart, but we are stronger than we realize. I know it's hard not to fall victim to fear, but we must try. Know that the royal court and many former villains are working together to protect Enchantasia. We simply ask that you remain patient."

Patient we will be, but for how long? That's what this reporter wants to know. (Although I'm told I can't get into that here, or we'd have to put this blog post on our opinion page.) For now, all I'll say is I hope the former Wicked Stepmother is right: someone needs to save us. The question is: Who?

◇◇◇◇◇◇◇

CURSE READINESS—HOW DO WE PREPARE?—*only in tomorrow's HEAS!*

SAVE THE RADISHES!

A Public Plea from the Enchantasia Farming Community

For months, our radish crops have been dwindling! We have appealed to the royal court and the Dwarf Police Squad for answers and have gotten nowhere.

Now we are asking the public to pitch a fork and help. If you see someone stealing radish plants, alert a farmer at once! If we aren't careful, radishes could disappear from our lives forever.

PAID FOR BY THE BRIAR PATCH
UNION OF ENCHANTASIA

Snail Mail

Don't trust the sharks!

Let sea snails deliver your mail safely!

FROM: Hayley Holliway at the coral
reef at Shipwreck Cove

TO: Gilly Cobbler at Fairy Tale Reform School

Gilly,

I'm not sure how fast this Snail Mail service is (they don't have Pegasus Postal Service in the ocean), but I had no choice but to try it out. I just wish upon a starfish that this message reaches you in time.

I think someone is trying to steal the magic lamp you sent me to protect and hide. I know it sounds strange, but I can feel a disturbance in the way the water flows, the fish move, and the wind blows. Trouble is brewing. Several ships have been spotted in the area. I haven't gotten close enough to see who they are (My mother only allows me to swim beyond the reef during the day. Sigh.), but I can tell they're searching for something. No one comes to Shipwreck Cove unless they want to get attacked by a kraken, and who wants to get attacked by a kraken? (Okay, so there's not really a kraken. Mermaids are just really good at telling tall tales.)

I've been under the sea a while now and don't know what's happening on land (I miss it), but my gills can sense danger. I fear it's You-Know-Who and his candy-loving squad. Come quickly, Gilly, and bring backup!

Your friend,
Hayley

CHAPTER 1

Ahoy, Matey!

Full speed ahead, me hearties!" Ollie shouts. He's got one hand on the pirate ship's wheel and the other holding a gold spyglass that he's looking through. "Land ho!"

"Land? Where exactly do you see land?" Jocelyn asks. Her pale face is almost green as she holds on to one of the ship's railings. The journey has been kind of rocky.

And I don't just mean the water, which is choppy. Our two days' voyage to Shipwreck Cove has been complicated by the fact that this ship has too many captains—Blackbeard, Ollie, and each of my friends has a different opinion on the fastest way to get to Hayley.

Professor Blackbeard agreed to take us on his ship, but neither he nor Madame Cleo, who offered to chaperone, had a map that showed the location of the cove. Apparently, they don't pinpoint secret mermaid coves on nautical charts. Ollie seems to think he's been there, though.

"Shipwreck Cove be straight ahead!" he says in a thick pirate brogue.

Allison Grace, who we call AG, narrows her blue eyes and looks out at the vast ocean in front of us. "I don't see anything," she whispers.

I shrug. "Neither do I."

"Ollie?" Kayla flies over, her fairy wings popping out and fluttering like they do whenever she's anxious. "I've been thinking a lot about Shipwreck Cove, and, um, doesn't the name make you think we should anchor elsewhere? I feel funny sailing the ship into a place that has 'shipwreck' in its name."

"I wouldn't worry about it yet," Jocelyn says, her cape billowing in the sea breeze. "Ollie's wrong—we are nowhere near land. A good sorceress like myself can tell."

Ollie's head swivels around so fast I'm sure it's going to spin off. "Are ye saying me be wrong? Do ye want to wind up in Davy Jones's locker?" Ollie asks the Evil Queen's younger sister. "If I say, 'There be land,' there be land ahead!"

The second Blackbeard asked Ollie to help him command his ship, Ollie went full pirate on us. He's wearing an eye patch even though we all know he has two brown eyes that he can see perfectly well out of, and he's swapped out his usual red bandanna for Blackbeard's wide black hat with a white feather stuck in the top.

I hear a *psst* and turn around.

"I think Ollie's saying that if Jocelyn questions him again, he'll make her walk the plank, which means throw her overboard," Maxine whispers to me and Jocelyn. She's been keeping a scroll of pirate terms and definitions so we can all understand Ollie's new pirate-speak.

Jocelyn narrows her eyes at Ollie, folding her arms across her chest. "I'd like to see him try."

Ollie is too busy singing a sea chantey to himself to pay her any mind. "All hands, ahoy! We be facing a kraken soon."

"A kraken?" Drool puddles around the edges of Maxine's ample ogre mouth. She links arms with Allison Grace, and they both look around nervously. "Gilly said that was just a myth."

"It *is* a myth," says Jax as he runs a sail effortlessly up one of the masts. The pirate ship's black skull-and-crossbones flag makes a snapping sound in the wind. (Jax has been battening and raising things like a pro, unlike the rest of us who haven't found our sea legs yet.) "Ollie, don't make them nervous."

"Nervous? Do I look nervous?" I take one of the arrows out of the quiver hanging from my back and aim it at the nothingness in front of us. "Why should any of us be nervous?"

"Yeah!" Jocelyn seconds, looking at Kayla, AG, and Maxine for backup. "Are you saying because we're girls, we can't hold our own against a mythical sea monster?"

"I said nothing of the sort." Jax flashes us a charming grin (his prince specialty). "We know our skills can't hold a candle to yours. Right, Ollie?"

Ollie doesn't answer. He's too busy licking his finger and holding it up in the wind. "Storm's a-brewing."

"There isn't a cloud in the sky!" Jocelyn argues.

"Shiver me timbers! Jocelyn, don't contradict the pirate captain," Maxine says, consulting her scroll. "You don't want to be...uh...shark bait!"

Ollie beams at her proudly.

Jocelyn rolls her eyes. "All I'm saying is we are nowhere near land, there is no storm coming, and Ollie has about as much knowledge of the seas as I have of what the Royal Ladies-in-Waiting do at club meetings."

"You're welcome to join us anytime," I say sweetly. "Our pink sash would coordinate well with your all-black ensemble." Jocelyn growls at me.

I may not love being a member of that club, but it is the one place at FTRS I can go without worrying Jocelyn will be there. She hates princess stuff more than I do.

"How we be doing, mateys?" The booming tread of Blackbeard's heavy, beat-up black boots announce his arrival on deck. (Pirates aren't much for the latest fashions. I can appreciate that.) "That be me hat you're sporting, Ollie?"

Ollie whips it off and laughs nervously. "Is it? How did that get there? I be losing me mind, Captain! Sorry!"

Blackbeard places it on his head, and the white feather on top starts to disintegrate. He nudges Ollie out of the way so he can take the wheel. "Madame Cleo says we be getting close to Shipwreck Cove."

"But sir, there is no land anywhere," Jax points out. "How can we be getting close?"

Blackbeard points a grimy black finger at his forehead. "We pirates see things with our minds. I know the sea like the back of me hands! We sense things mere landlubbers like yerselves do not!"

"Darlings!" I hear Madame Cleo's voice. We all look over the side of the ship and see the sea siren sporting long, canary-yellow hair. (Yesterday it was green.) She smiles beatifically. "How are you feeling, AG? Get your sea legs yet?"

"Not really." AG clutches her stomach. "But still glad you convinced my mom and dad to let me come."

"Of course, darling!" Madame Cleo says, and her hair goes from yellow to pink. "That Beast of a father of yours is a real softy when you talk to him the right way. Besides, Beauty agreed you need a chance to spread your wings." AG beams at her. "Did Ollie and Beardy-Boy tell you I spoke to three puffer fish and a school of seahorses that said Shipwreck Cove is two nautical miles ahead?"

"See things with your mind, huh?" Jocelyn mutters. Blackbeard's cheeks take on a pink tinge.

"Thanks, Madame Cleo!" I shout. "I'll tell the others." I pull the broken mirror out of the sheath hanging from my side and hold it into the sunlight. The broken glass practically blinds me. The gold leaf on the handle is etched away, and the binds holding it together are fragile at best, but Professor

Harlow's mirror—once used so she could communicate with Alva, the Wicked Fairy of Sleeping Beauty's nightmares—has been magically restored.

Two black eyes stare back at me. "Yes, Ms. Cobbler, what do you need now?" the former Evil Queen drawls.

"Professor Harlow, we—" I start to say.

Harlow cuts me off. "Honestly, Flora, if the girl can't make a single decision on her own, how can we really keep her in the Magical Metamorphosis Program here at school? She's not acting like a leader should. Now, Jocelyn on the other hand…"

"Harlow, please be reasonable," Headmistress Flora says wearily.

I can't remember the last time I saw the former Wicked Stepmother look this tired. Actually, I do remember—it was when we snuck out of FTRS and climbed a beanstalk to find my younger sister Anna and got tricked by Rumpelstiltskin. Or maybe it was when Maxine made a wish on the magic lamp we're now looking for, and it made everyone at FTRS go bananas. Or maybe…

"Gillian? Gilly? Are you listening to me?"

"Sorry, Headmistress Flora. Yes!" I had zoned out again.

Ollie is right about the sea being good for collecting your thoughts. The minute I stepped aboard, all I could think about was Anna. Is she truly evil? Or under Rumpelstiltskin's spell? Does it even matter? If she's trying to hurt Enchantasia, she's evil. And that means we're on opposite sides.

"Hayley sent the letter to Gilly; therefore Gilly is in control of the mirror on this trip," Flora tells Harlow.

"Yes, but Ms. Cobbler can be so needy!" Harlow argues. "Every two seconds she seems to command me to come to this mirror, and you know I don't do well with commands, especially when Angelina and I are so busy trying to decipher clues about when Stiltskin will launch this curse."

"I believe Ms. Cobbler has only called for you once," Professor Wolfington's voice is as calm as ever as he strokes his long beard. "And if all we've read about Shipwreck Cove is true, this is the time when the crew will need us. The cove is clouded—literally—in mystery so it will take all of our minds to find it and make sure you have safe passage."

"Safe passage?" AG repeats, looking as green as Jocelyn. "Why wouldn't they let us enter? We're friends, not foes!"

"Allison Grace, are you feeling all right?" Beauty slides into the frame with a concerned smile. "You look green, dear. How are all of you holding up? So brave! I'm very proud of you."

"She should have stayed home," Professor Sebastian growls.

"Father!" AG groans.

"You are hundreds of nautical miles away!" our sometimes Beast-of-a-professor reminds her. "How can we protect any of you if you encounter Rumpelstiltskin on the high seas?"

"We're going to beat him to the lamp," I say, willing it to be true. "We have to because if we don't, he'll use that lamp to get the final ingredients for his curse." There'll be no stopping him from erasing the Enchantasia we know—and all of us in it—so that he can take the kingdom over. I can't let that happen.

"Madame Cleo says Shipwreck Cove is only a few nautical miles ahead," Kayla tells Professor Sebastian.

"And we haven't seen anyone out here but us, so maybe those other ships Hayley mentioned didn't find anything and left!" Maxine says excitedly.

Jocelyn jostles for position in front of the mirror. "But I don't see land anywhere, sister! I think they're all wrong!"

"We're not! Me smell a storm coming!" Ollie is jumping up and down behind Maxine and Jocelyn to be seen. I struggle to hold the mirror steady. The choppy waves have only gotten worse, and the wind has definitely picked up.

"Maybe Ollie is right," I start to say just as I see something jut out of the water off the bow of the ship. "What's that in the water?"

"Rocks!" Ollie shouts. He rushes over to the pirate wheel and grabs it out of Blackbeard's hands.

Blackbeard looks through his spyglass. "Boulders! Be right ahead!"

We make a hard right that sends Maxine tumbling sideways, and I stick the mirror back in my sheath so it doesn't fall. Kayla tries to fly, but the wind holds her down. The rest of us grab on to a mast.

"We're going to crash!" AG cries.

Ollie keeps turning, but the jagged, black rocks seem to be growing right in front of my eyes, spreading like wildflowers and forming a barricade in the middle of the ocean. How can that be? They weren't there two minutes ago!

"What do we do?" Maxine cries.

"Steer steady, matey!" Blackbeard instructs Ollie as we all brace for impact. "Get more wind in your sails, Jax! We must stay the course!"

"Stay the course?" I question, but Blackbeard isn't listening. He's too busy using his spyglass to view the path ahead. I look over the side for Madame Cleo, but she's disappeared.

"Aye, aye, Captain!" Jax jumps off the top deck and begins raising and lowering sails.

"Captain? He doesn't call me 'captain,'" I hear Ollie grumble as he struggles against the wind to hold the wheel steady.

"We're doomed! If only I were in charge we wouldn't be sailing straight into a rock," Jocelyn rails against the sudden clouds in the sky.

But her voice fades away as a gust of wind nearly knocks us all off the top deck. The ship veers right, then left, swinging side to side like a bottle about to fall off a table. The sun disappears behind a group of clouds, and a shadow falls across the ship. The hair on the back of my neck stands up.

"What is going on? We can't see!" I hear Professor Harlow's muffled voice coming from the mirror hung at my side.

I pull the mirror out, look into it, and smile. Harlow's nose is practically pressed against the glass. "Sorry! Don't want to bother you unless it's necessary. We'll let you know when there is something to see." I put the mirror back into my sheath.

"Miss Cobbler! Miss Cobbler!" I hear her yelling.

"Captain, we be about to crash!" Ollie shouts to Blackbeard.

"Steady!" Blackbeard insists.

"I'm not the best swimmer," Maxine cries as she clings to both me and the mast. "What are we going to do?"

"Steady!" Blackbeard shouts again.

I can see there is no arguing with him. "We stick together," I tell Maxine, looping my arm through hers. "Friends for life."

She gives me a toothy grin. "Friends for life!"

We hold tight to the pole as the ship bounces along, the mermaid figurehead of Madame Cleo on the bow inching closer to our rocky demise.

"Steady!" Blackbeard continues to shout as the wind begins to howl.

Ollie does as he's told, even if he closes his eye that isn't covered by a patch. I clutch Maxine's meaty arm tighter as the ship hits the first rock...and rolls right through it.

"Ha-ha!" Blackbeard shouts triumphantly. "It be a mirage! I be right!"

"Well done, Captain!" Ollie says as we sail through the rocks without incident.

We're so busy cheering and hugging one another that no one notices fog as thick as the cafeteria's pea soup rolling in around us. There is no wind, no sound, just the boat gliding as if it's flying. It's the perfect kind of weather for a sneak attack, which makes me nervous. I'm on guard, waiting for something to jump out of the ocean at us. Still, I trust Blackbeard. He knew the rocks were phony. Soon the fog begins to lift, the sky is blue once more, and in the distance, I see the green landscape of a small island. Turquoise-blue water surrounds a beach with tons of palm trees.

"Shipwreck Cove straight ahead, Captain!" Ollie shouts and we cheer again.

"There it be, my fair lass!" Blackbeard tells us as he waves to Madame Cleo, who is on a rock not far from shore.

She must have swam ahead. And she's not alone! Several mermaids are sunning themselves on the rock with her. I wish I had a spyglass like Blackbeard so I could see if one of the mermaids is Hayley.

I guess they call this place Shipwreck Cove to scare sailors away because, to be honest, the place looks like paradise. No wonder Hayley missed home. It's beautiful! The sun feels warm on my face, the water is so clear you can see the fish swimming beneath it, and the island looks peaceful.

"Darlene must love it here!" Maxine gushes. "If she's left her magic lamp long enough to see it."

"I can't wait to go swimming!" AG says as if we're on a vacation, which in a way, I guess we are. Hanging out with mermaids for a few days in their secret cove does sound fun.

Jocelyn frowns. "I hope I made enough of my homemade sunscreen. I tend to burn."

Jax appears at my side. "Yeah, we wouldn't want her bursting into flames," he whispers, and we both giggle quietly.

"Full speed ahead to Shipwreck Cove!" Ollie says happily.

I breathe in the sea air and feel my body start to relax.

Suddenly, the deck pitches so far to the right, I'm sure we're going to capsize. Maxine and Kayla scream as the ship comes to a crashing halt in the middle of the water.

Jax lets go of my arm and looks at Ollie. "What happened? Did we hit a rock?"

Ollie's face darkens. "No. It's almost as if…"

"As if what?" I shout, but my voice is drowned out by my own scream as a giant tentacle slams across the deck and tries to pull the ship under.

CHAPTER 2

Kraken Up

K raken!" Ollie shouts as Blackbeard raises a sword from his sheath and begins running at one of the giant tentacles slithering across the deck.

"Everybody move!" Jax shouts as more tentacles begin climbing up onto the deck. The fleshy limbs are covered in slimy suction cups with rows of teeth.

"Defend yer ship before it pulls us under, mateys!" Blackbeard stabs a tentacle and it recoils. There is lots of shouting out commands as the crew swipes at the tentacles with their swords. Ollie, meanwhile, is desperately trying to get the ship to move and not succeeding.

"But you said they were just a myth!" Maxine shouts as a tentacle comes dangerously close to hitting her in the back.

"Because that's what Hayley said in her letter!" I pull Maxine out of the way and look for something to defend ourselves with. Doesn't Blackbeard have a cannon on this thing? Yes! I pull Maxine up the steps to the higher end of the deck where the cannon is. "None of this is real."

A tentacle hits one of the ship's masts, and it crashes to the deck with a loud thud.

"Looks pretty real to me," Kayla says, using her wand to send a spray of sparks at the nearest tentacle. We hear a withering shriek, and the tentacle disappears over the side of the ship.

"It's working!" AG says happily. But seconds later, the tentacle shoots out of the water again and comes right for us. Maxine, Kayla, and I dive out of the way.

"Get to the cannon," I tell them and we spring up, running as fast as we can past Jocelyn.

"Take that, you giant, smelly squid!" she cries as she tosses fireball after fireball at the creature with little effect. "Not enough? Well, how do you like this?" She begins to mouth something I can't hear and raises her hand to the tentacle nearest her. The tentacle begins to shimmer and glow and then bursts into hundreds of butterflies. "*Ha!*"

The rest of us cheer. Maybe Jocelyn can turn the whole Kraken into a giant butterfly. That wouldn't be too tough to fight, would it?

The butterflies suddenly fall to the floor and transform into hundreds of tiny tentacles that start to grow.

"Move back! Move back!" Blackbeard tells us, using his sword to send the tiny tentacles flying off the side of the ship. "Ollie, me matey! Get ye ship moving, or we are going to wind up in Davy Jones's locker!"

"*Ah-whoo!*" I hear a wolf growl and look over. Allison Grace has transformed into her beastly form. She leaps high into the air in her pink party dress and clings to the tentacle, biting into it with her sharp, daggerlike teeth. The tentacle swings back and forth, trying to shake her off, then disappears over the side of the ship.

"AG!" I scream as Kayla flies past me.

"I've got her!" Kayla shouts, nimbly dodging the beast as she flies right, left, then dives low. She pulls AG up out of the water and starts flying toward the island. At least the two of them are—

"*Gilly!*" Jax plows into me, knocking me to the deck. I slide across the wet surface and crash into the bow, looking up in time to see Jax get plucked by a tentacle that apparently was about to snatch me. It twists itself around him and pulls him into the air.

"*Jax!*" I scramble to get up, slipping and sliding across the deck as I race toward the beast before it disappears in the water with Jax in its clutches. "*Jax!*" My heart is pounding as I try to reach him.

Jocelyn sees what's happening and starts firing orbs at the tentacle, almost striking Jax in the thigh.

"Watch where you're aiming!" Jax shouts.

"Sorry! Just trying to help you live!" Jocelyn fires back.

"Hang on!" I shout to Jax.

"I'm trying!" Jax pounds at the tentacle, willing it to unwind its tight grasp.

The ship lists again, tossing us all across the deck.

"I think I got the anchor free!" Ollie shouts. "Or someone did!"

"It be me lady!" Blackbeard runs past me, slicing two tentacles in half with his sword. "She has the mermaids helping her. I can hear her siren song!"

I can't hear anything in all this commotion, but I'm almost to the top of the deck where I can reach Jax. The tentacle is swinging wildly, trying to avoid Jocelyn's flaming orbs. I dive under one and can almost reach Jax's leg. He sees me and his eyes widen.

"Gilly, stay back!" he says, struggling against the tentacle's hold.

"And watch you become fish food?" I grab one of the pulleys on the deck and race to the mast. I hoist myself to the top. "I don't think so!"

"I just saved you! You getting caught right now would kind of defeat the whole purpose!" Jax shouts, trying to kick out from the squid's suction-cup tentacles.

"That's what you're worried about?" I slide across the mast's horizontal yard, trying to hang on as the ship veers to its side again.

"I don't need saving!" Jax goes flying back in the grasp of the tentacles.

"Looks like you do!" I yell as I pull myself up and stand on the yard.

BOOM!

I see the cannonball fly through the air at the kraken and hit one of the tentacles. I cheer as the kraken screeches, and the tentacles begin to writhe. The one holding Jax releases him, and he starts to free-fall to the water below. But at the last second, another tentacle grabs him and begins to pull him under the choppy water.

"No!" I grab the rope and start to slide down the mast, but by the time I hit the deck, Jax is gone. The others race to the side of the ship.

"I don't see him!" Maxine cries.

"*Jax! Jax!*" I shout, but I know he can't hear me underwater. "We have to do something!"

"We'll get pulled under if we stay here!" Ollie tells me. "We'll send the mermaids to find him."

"But it will be too late!" I argue.

As the ship starts to move away, I see the tentacles emerge from the water again. I climb onto the ship's railing and prepare to jump, but someone pulls me back.

"What are you doing?" Jocelyn shouts. "You'll get pulled under!"

"But Jax is down there!" I cry, starting to feel panicked. I've already lost Anna. I can't lose Jax too. He was my first true friend at FTRS. I pull my uniform skirt out of Jocelyn's grasp, and she grabs it again. We are yanking and pulling at each other when we hear Maxine scream.

"Look! It's Jax!"

Jocelyn and I lean over the railing. Jax's head is bobbing up and down in the water. He appears unconscious, but someone is keeping him afloat. It's Hayley! She sees me and motions toward shore. I'm so relieved, I could cry, but then I spy the kraken moving like a giant wave just below the surface.

"The sea beast be headed back! Get to yer positions!" Blackbeard shouts.

"Hayley and Jax are going to be swallowed up," Maxine yells.

And that's when I hear the most beautiful sound I've ever heard. It sounds like bells tinkling, a waterfall rushing, and children laughing all rolled into one. But it's none of those things. It's actually a single voice. Madame Cleo's!

"Me lady! You be all right!" Blackbeard cries, looking at Madame Cleo bobbing in the water a few yards away. She isn't alone. There is a wall of merfolk with her, and they're all singing the same lullaby. I feel my eyes drifting closed as Maxine snores next to me. She sounds like a wall about to crumble. As my eyes start to close, I see the kraken's tentacles slowly drifting below the surface before everything goes black.

When I awake, someone is standing over me, their face blocked out by the sun.

"Hey there, thief."

"Jax!" I sit up, feeling sand slip through my fingers. Somehow I'm lying on a beach. We've somehow made it to Shipwreck Cove's shore. And Jax is all right. "I thought..." I'm so overcome with emotion, I don't know what to say as he pulls me to standing.

"You were worried, I know." He flashes me a charming smile, and I feel my cheeks start to burn. "I told you I had it covered."

Someone behind us clears their throat. "Actually, *I* had it covered."

"Hayley!" I throw my arms around my half-mermaid friend, thrilled for the distraction. Hayley's in human form again, looking tan with almost white-blond hair from all her time in the sun. "There was a kraken! You saved Jax!" I turn and look at Jax. "And I wasn't worried about you."

He flicks a patch of sand off his wet uniform shirt. "You were worried."

"It's all right," Hayley tells me, sounding calm. "Everyone is okay. Kayla and AG made it to shore, the kraken has been charmed back to sleep, and the ship only has minor damage."

I look around. Blackbeard's ship is anchored behind me, and Ollie and Blackbeard are making repairs while Madame Cleo suns herself on a nearby rock, playing hostess to a group of mermaids. Jocelyn, Kayla, and AG are putting up a pop-up castle on the beach, and there are lots of people milling about. Everyone seems unusually calm.

"You said in your letter the kraken was just a myth," I accuse her.

"Well," Hayley shrugs. "I couldn't be *completely* honest with you over Snail Mail. Snails aren't known for being brave, and if my note was compromised, I'd be giving away Shipwreck Cove's biggest secret."

"But we almost got destroyed," I point out.

"You wouldn't have been if Kirk was behaving," Hayley tells me.

"Kirk?"

"That's the name of the kraken," Jax supplies. "Apparently he's the mermaids' pet."

"Some pet," I grumble.

"He's great. He keeps all the ships away when they slip

through the fog barrier, but today…" Her face clouds over. "He was under a spell we couldn't control."

I inhale sharply. "Rumpelstiltskin?"

Hayley nods, and I notice her eyes are teary. "He was here. Just a few hours before you. We couldn't hold him off. Kirk was under a spell and…" Her voice fades away.

"He had all of Hayley's family cornered, but Madame Cleo helped her free them from an underwater cave while we were battling the kraken," Jax tells me. "That's why it took them so long to get to the surface and sing Kirk their lullaby. Stiltskin and Alva bewitched it."

"Where are they now?" I whisper.

"Long gone," Jax says grimly. "And they've got Darlene."

I sink down onto the sand again and hear Maxine sniffling as she walks over with Kayla, Jocelyn, and AG.

"You told her?" Maxine asks Jax, who nods. "I feel terrible." Maxine is drooling badly. "Darlene is such a good genie. She wouldn't hurt a soul, but in Stiltskin's hands, we're done for. She doesn't stand a chance against him tied up in her lamp!"

We're all quiet, the realization of Maxine's words sinking in. We've lost the battle before we even got started.

Rumpelstiltskin is probably casting his curse as we speak. I inhale sharply, waiting for the world in front of me to swirl and disappear with a pop. I stare at Ollie, who has his eyes closed as if he's thinking the same thing.

Ollie opens his eyes and looks at the rest of us. "Okay, why isn't the curse happening? If he has Darlene and three wishes to make, why hasn't he made them yet?"

"I don't know." Why hasn't he cast his curse if he has wishes at his disposal?

"Darlene told us she can't grant evil wishes. That's why," Maxine says.

"Yeah, but Stiltskin would find a way around that, wouldn't he?" I ask, and we're all quiet again.

Haley pulls something out of her pocket. It's a small brown-and-white conch shell. "Maybe this will explain everything."

"I'm not sure putting a shell to our ears and listening to the ocean right now is going to help," Jocelyn says bitterly.

"Not that!" Hayley rolls her eyes. "Geez, that's such an ocean stereotype—hearing the sound of the ocean in a shell. No, when Stiltskin found Darlene and became her master, she had this shell in her hands. I arrived just as he ordered Darlene back into her lamp, and this shell fell to the floor.

She looked right at me as she dropped it and said, 'Tell Maxine I'm sorry.'"

Maxine starts to audibly cry, and huge, fat tears fall onto the sand. "She thinks I blame her! Oh, Darlene! You don't need to apologize to me!" She takes the shell from Hayley and holds it close to her heart.

"There has to be a reason she had a shell and dropped it," I reason. "I've never seen Darlene leave items outside her lamp before."

"She's no litterer, that's true." Maxine sniffs. "Maybe the shell is a message."

"I thought of that," admits Hayley, whose eyes shift to Jocelyn, then downward. "But when I put the shell to my ear, there was no sound."

"Oh, so maybe the shell-to-the-ear technique isn't so ridiculous after all!" Jocelyn says.

"Did you rub it?" AG asks. "Like you would a lamp?"

Hayley's eyes widen. "I didn't think of that." She takes the shell from Maxine and rubs it. Nothing happens.

"What a waste of my last few minutes in the kingdom," Jocelyn mutters. "That curse is going to fall on us any second now!"

"Maybe the only way the message works is if *Maxine* rubs the shell," I guess. "The message could be just for her since she's one of Darlene's former masters."

Maxine cocks her head to one side. "You think?"

"Of course!" AG says. "She loved you!"

Maxine grins. "We did have a strong bond."

Jax hands the shell to Maxine, who turns it over in her large hands. As soon as she rubs the top of the shell, a long, steady stream of smoke emerges from the opening in the conch shell. The smoke slowly transforms into Darlene; big, red hair, bright-gold dress, hoop earrings, and all. She looks like she's ready for a night out on the genie town.

"Darlene!" Maxine cries. "You moved from your lamp to a shell. That's so smart!"

Darlene blinks, looks both ways worriedly, then back at Maxine. "Maxine, I don't have much time. Rumpelstiltskin has found Shipwreck Cove, and he's searching for me as I speak. Any moment, I'll be ripped from my lamp and have to accept that evil little troll as my new master, so listen carefully."

"Cool! I want to learn to leave hidden messages in shells," Ollie whispers, and the rest of us shush him.

"I'm afraid I have some bad news, dollface," Darlene

says, her ghostly pale complexion looking even whiter than usual. "I lied to you about the genie rules. I know what you're thinking: 'Darlene would never lie to me!'"

"Darlene would never lie to me!" Maxine repeats.

"But I did," the genie adds.

Jocelyn whistles. "Uh-oh."

"It's true you only get three wishes, but beyond that, all the wish rules are my own," Darlene says. "Why is that a problem? Because Rumpelstiltskin is about to become my master."

"But you said you can't grant evil wishes," Maxine says as drool runs down her mouth.

"Yes, yes, I know I said genies can't grant evil wishes, but that's more like a standard I set for myself. Not a hard-and-fast rule." Darlene puts one hand on her hip, or where it would be if she weren't all smoke. "I am a classy genie, and as a personal rule, I don't grant malevolent wishes. Who wants to grant a wish to destroy the kingdom? But as I said, it's not a law. It's more like a genie code of honor."

"Oh no. Oh no. Oh no," AG starts to hyperventilate, and I notice hair begin to grow on her face. She's so upset, she's going to transform again. I rub her back to calm her down.

"All is not lost, however: to try to make all genies follow the same code of honor, the genie council passed a law that says if a genie grants evil wishes, no matter what the extenuating circumstances, their powers will slowly diminish with each wish."

"See, we're fine!" Maxine says, wiping sweat from her brow. "Darlene would never want to lose her powers."

"But, if Rumpelstiltskin gets ahold of me, I know he'll try to bend me to his will." She frowns. "And if I grant three evil wishes, I'll be banished from my genie community, and I do *not* want that to happen. I certainly don't want to live in a world run by Rumpelstiltskin either, so please, find a way to get my lamp back before any of these things happen."

"How are we going to do that?" Jocelyn asks. "He's already gone!"

"Even if we could find him immediately, Stiltskin could still spend his wishes before we get there and give Alva the lamp to make three more," Jax adds.

I groan. "I didn't even think of that possibility."

"I'll do my best stall," Darlene tells us. "I'll try to throw some smoke and mirrors his way and try to keep his wishes in check. Hayley told me about the curse he wants to cast, and wowza, it's a doozy. We can only hope he'll believe my lies about not being allowed to cast evil wishes. But if not, at least we know he can't cast the curse until—"

Darlene's image vanishes into thin air.

CHAPTER 3

Fairy Uncertain

U ntil when?" I cry. "Bring the message back!"

Maxine shakes the shell and taps the top. "Darlene? Darlene?" There is no response. "Where is the rest of the message?" she asks Hayley.

Hayley's face is grim. "That must have been all she got to say before Rumpelstiltskin summoned her from the lamp."

I look at the others in horror. "Darlene said Stiltskin couldn't cast the curse until…when? How did she know a date for the curse and we don't?"

"I'm not sure." Jax scratched his head. "But she sounded certain, didn't she?"

"She did," I say, feeling defeated. "Now what?"

Jax looks at Hayley. "Who was with Stiltskin when he came?"

"The Stiltskin Squad." She glances at me apprehensively. "Including Anna." She twists her hands uncomfortably. "She said you two made up and I believed her. She was the one who tricked me into letting her onshore, and then she held my family captive."

My heart starts to beat wildly, and I close my eyes to try to block out what I know to be true. My sister is a villain now. "I'm so sorry, Hayley."

"It's not your fault," she says, squeezing my hand. "I should have known when she came without you that something was wrong. She was cagey when I asked about you. I guess I just wanted to believe—"

"That she was good," I finish because I have felt the same way in the past. "I know."

Hayley holds her head in her hands, her bleached-blond hair spilling around her fingers. "I can't believe I let them take Darlene and the lamp."

"We will get the lamp back. The important thing is, you're safe and your family is all right." Kayla puts her arm around Hayley.

"Still, Mom doesn't feel safe in Shipwreck Cove now that Rumpelstiltskin knows where we are and has the lamp. She's worried about the curse. We all are," Hayley tells us. "My brother is a mess. He keeps saying things that are unnerving my parents."

I notice a small boy who is Hayley's clone is walking around in circles nearby. He seems like he's in some sort of trance. "The curse is coming," I hear him say. "The curse can't be stopped." I feel chills run down my spine.

"Now what?" Jocelyn asks us. "That evil little villain has his hands on a magic lamp, and there is a curse deadline we had no clue about. Anyone else think we should focus on getting out of this cove and find him?"

"We'll never catch him with our ship like that." Ollie gestures to the splintered mess of our pirate ship. "It's going to take at least a day or two till we can set sail again."

Everyone is quiet. I can hear Madame Cleo telling a story about Stiltskin to the other mermaids, but I can't listen. I suddenly feel so doomed.

"Gillian? Gillian? Ms. Cobbler, where are you?" I hear a muffled voice and look down.

The mirror! It's still in my sheath, covered in a ton of

sand and seaweed, but it's glowing. I pluck the pieces of seaweed off it and stare into the hazy glass.

All of my professors are staring back at me. Beauty bursts into tears.

"For the love of Grimm, where were you?" Harlow snaps. "When we saw the kraken and heard the commotion we thought the worst!"

"Is everyone all right?" Beauty asks, and the others crowd around.

"We're okay, Mother," AG tells her. "But Rumpelstiltskin was here before us. He got the lamp, then put a hex on Kirk, who attacked our ship."

"Who is Kirk?" Professor Sebastian demands.

"The kraken," Jax explains. "Apparently he's normally friendly."

"Who names a kraken Kirk?" Flora mutters.

"I told you Stiltskin would beat us to the lamp!" Harlow snaps at the others. "There will be no stopping him now."

"Getting hysterical is not going to help us," I hear Professor Wolfington say. "There is still hope."

"Hope is dwindling!" Professor Sebastian roars, and

Harlow seems to agree with him. Suddenly they're all shouting and arguing, and it's hard to understand what's going on. Finally, I hear someone whistle.

"Everyone calm down!" Flora runs a hand through her salt-and-pepper hair. "Now, Gillian, tell us what happened. Calmly. *And without interruption*," she adds for Harlow and Professor Sebastian's benefit.

I do the best I can, explaining about the kraken and Hayley's family and the lost lamp and Darlene's attempt to give us the deadline. My teachers are stunned into silence.

"He's waiting for a Fire Moon," someone says softly.

"Mother!" Kayla touches the mirror in my outstretched hands. "It's good to see you up and about."

"Hello, darling," Angelina says.

Kayla's mom is the fairy that was predestined to write Rumpelstiltskin's story. She has been in hiding ever since Stiltskin lifted his curse on her and allowed her to return to human form.

"What is a Fire Moon?" I ask.

"It's when there are three new moons in one month, which is extremely rare," Angelina tells us. "The third new moon, instead of being invisible to the eye like a normal new moon, casts a reddish shadow over the land. It's said Fire Moons signify danger and darkness looming. Fairies usually hibernate on such occasions." Her face is grim. "The last one was before I was born, but I remember my mother talking about it. Many dark curses throughout history have been cast during these celestial events—they offer optimal conditions—but they only occur every fifty years or so."

"When will the next one occur?" Even Harlow sounds anxious.

We watch through the mirror as Angelina goes to her star charts. "This can't be right." When she looks up, I see her face is full of fear. "The next one is in three days." She clutches the gem around her neck. "How did I not see this coming?"

My heart begins to thump wildly. We only have three days left to beat Rumpelstiltskin at his own game, or the world as we know it will be over.

Flora looks at the others. "We need to shore up the school's defenses. We cannot let him get his final curse ingredient—the harp."

"He won't! The harp is hidden at FTRS," Kayla says brightly. "It's safe."

Harlow's face is grim. "We thought the lamp was safe too."

"The lamp isn't an ingredient in the spell," Professor Sebastian reminds the others. "It's just unfortunate that he has such a powerful weapon at his disposal. A genie is a good ally to have in a war like this."

"Poor Darlene!" Maxine mutters. "If only I had left her on the shelf in that shoppe."

"Someone explain what he needs to cast the curse again," Ollie says. "How does it work?"

"In addition to the perfect time and place, it appears he needs a golden egg," Angelina begins.

"Which he has. Gilly gave him one," Jocelyn says.

"And Alva—" Angelina begins.

"Whom Gilly woke when Anna tricked her into singing with the harp," Maxine says.

"Thanks for the reminder." I'm feeling worse by the second.

"Then there is fairy blood," Angelina adds. "Plus the harp."

"Alva is a fairy. They can't use hers?" Kayla asks.

Angelina purses her lips. "The curse isn't that simple. He

won't want to spill any of Alva's. She's his true love. He'd protect her, but he does need fairy blood and I fear…"

"No, you're safe here," Harlow insists. "So is the harp. Madame Cleo hid it with magic herself. Where is Cleo?"

"We'll bring you over to her." My arms and legs feel heavy as I walk across the sand to the rock where Blackbeard and Madame Cleo are hanging out as if they don't have a care in the world. "Madame Cleo?" I ask. "The professors want to know if the harp pieces are safe."

Madame Cleo's hair cascades in purple waves down her back. Her fin is currently the same color as the clamshells she has on as a top. "Oh yes, darling! Very safe!"

"See? Me lady is a good one at hiding treasure," Blackbeard says adoringly.

"How do you know the harp is safe?" Harlow's voice is droll as she pets the raven that has landed on her shoulder. Is that Aldo? I can't remember the last time I saw him.

"Because…well…because…" Cleo's cheeks flush pink, and soon her scales and hair are a similar shade. "Because I don't even remember where I hid them."

"Fairy be," Professor Sebastian mutters under his breath.

I feel the panic start to rise immediately. Madame Cleo

sometimes suffers from short-term memory loss on account of zapping herself once when she was trying to go after the Little Mermaid.

"But I know it was an excellent hiding spot!" Madame Cleo says brightly. "So you see, it's really for the best. If I don't remember, how could anyone else find them?"

"Cleo, we can't not know where they are!" Harlow snaps.

"I do know! I just can't recall where they are *at the moment.*"

The two start bickering. We back away as Cleo's hair turns a violent shade of red.

"If she's lost the harp, maybe Stiltskin has already gotten his hands on it," Jax says. "If he has the harp, then…"

"He's going to get the other *things* he needs too," I realize. "And if he needs fairy blood, couldn't he use my sister's? She has fairy ancestry."

"Yeah, but she hasn't shown any sort of fairy ability, has she?" Kayla asks. "No one in your family has, right? Fairy blood in a curse has to be strong, and someone who doesn't even know they're a fairy wouldn't be strong. Anna should be safe."

Safe or a threat? I'm not sure what to think. I don't know who my sister is anymore.

"But what about Kayla and her family?" Ollie asks, and I freeze.

"I don't think he'd harm my mother. He needs her to write his book," Kayla says. "And if he messes with me and my sisters, she will fight him. He must be looking for someone else's…someone specific."

"But who?" I wonder aloud. We're all quiet.

Kayla flutters next to Ollie and places her head on his shoulder. "What if we don't even know each other in the new Enchantasia?"

"Know each other?" Ollie asks. "What if we don't even exist? Fairy Tale Reform School probably won't."

Jocelyn sits down on a nearby mossy rock. "I'm sure I'll exist. Being the sister of a former villain and all, I suspect I'd be useful."

"No one is disappearing," Jax insists as Maxine begins to wail.

"What are we going to do?" AG asks.

I want to say I don't know because it's true. I don't. We've been down and out before, but never this badly. If Stiltskin has everything he needs, how can we stop him? *Think like a villain, Gilly*, I tell myself. *If you were him, what would you be doing right now?*

"Gillian!" Blackbeard is waving the mirror frantically in the air as Madame Cleo dives off her rock and disappears below the surface. "They be wanting you again! All of you lads and lassies, come here!" We race back to the rock. "Madame Cleo has gone off with Hayley and a few of the mermaids to look for the harp," Blackbeard explains. "Hayley says she'll be catching up with you all soon. Er, she didn't want to keep me lady waiting."

Madame Cleo did not look happy earlier. I don't blame her.

"But the professors be wanting to talk to you all before they get to work." Blackbeard holds out the mirror.

I warily accept it. Every one of my teachers is squeezed in front of the mirror again.

"Madame Cleo is going to find the harp pieces," Headmistress Flora tells me efficiently. "You are *not* to help her look. Hayley and some other merfolk are going to do that."

"What if he wishes for the pieces in the meantime?" AG asks.

"I would think if he did, we would know immediately," Flora says, "so we will proceed as if Darlene is doing everything in her power to make sure that doesn't happen."

"So should we just sail back to school?" Ollie asks.

"No," Harlow jumps in. "You are to accompany Gilly to visit her grandmother."

My grandmother? "Rumpelstiltskin is about to enact a curse that will erase Enchantasia as we know it, and you want me to visit my grandmother?"

Harlow narrows her eyes at me. "Don't be fresh with me, young lady. Why, I could—"

Beauty steps in between us. "I think Gillian is asking how this is the best use of her limited time."

"Exactly!" I pipe up.

"This type of curse will require fairy blood with just the right properties," Angelina explains to me. "The book tells me he's still looking to acquire fairy blood, which is odd considering he has your sister and Alva. He'd never harm her, or your sister, but more likely she isn't showing any sort of fairy abilities. So whose blood does he need if not mine?" I notice her glance quickly at Harlow. "Since we can't leave the school with everything going on, we are tasking you with talking to someone in the fairy community who might understand what type of fairy blood he's looking for."

I'm still skeptical. "And you think my reclusive grandmother might know?" I am almost positive I catch a passing glance between my professors before Sebastian speaks.

"As someone with fairy ancestry, with a fairy grandmother who has been around a long time, you might be able to gain insight on what Stiltskin needs, with her help." He pauses. "Perhaps having fairy blood within you can also help stop him."

"How? I've never exhibited any kind of fairy magic."

"You were able to open a villain book, and only villains can normally do that," Kayla reminds me.

That's true. "But why my grandmother? There's no other fairy I could speak with who lives closer?"

Harlow and Angelina look at each other again. Then Angelina speaks. "There is something I haven't mentioned before. The book's ending involves your family. You are somehow tied up in this curse, Gillian—or your family is—in a way I don't understand yet."

I feel too shaky to speak. I'm not sure if it's because I'm nervous or I'm finally getting used to being on dry land again, and now I'm about to get back on a boat. I didn't even get a chance to meet Hayley's family, explore her paradise, or see Kirk the kraken as a friendly pet rather than a foe. Everything feels as if it's moving so fast, and I want time to slow down. But not rewind, of course. "I'm guess I'm going to meet my grandmother then."

"We will all go with her," Jax speaks up, and the others nod.

Professor Wolfington smiles. "We were hoping you'd say that. We need Blackbeard back here to help Cleo…search. She responds well to him."

Blackbeard burps and blushes. "Me lady and I are like a pirate and the sea. Intertwined! We will work 'round the clock to get me ship ready. Ollie, you command it. I trust her with you. I'll find another way back."

Ollie bows. "Thank you, sir! I'm a true captain! Can I borrow your hat?"

Blackbeard's smile fades. "No."

"This sounds fun!" Maxine interrupts. "Meeting Gilly's family? Going on another trip together? I always wanted to vacation with my friends."

"I've always wanted to go anywhere without my parents!" AG gushes. "No offense, Father."

Everyone is much more excited than I'd expect them to be about coming on a trip to see my grandma.

A grandma I've never met and who has never tried to reach out to me.

Yes, this sounds like loads of fun.

Professor Sebastian clears his throat. "This trip is not a vacation. It's important work." We all nod. "Since you'll be spending so much time outside class, I'm giving you a mid-term assignment to do while you're at sea."

We all groan.

"You want us to do homework *now*? When a villain is threatening to rewrite history as we know it?" Jax asks.

"Yes!" Professor Sebastian does not sound apologetic in the slightest. "Evil will always try to stop us. That doesn't mean we stop living. Your mini magical scrolls will update with the assignment shortly."

I hear a tinkling of bells. Maxine already has her mini scroll unrolled. "Ooh! 'Five years from now I will be…'? Such a fun topic!"

"Five years from now, we'll all be erased," Jocelyn says, and we all sort of laugh. It's not funny, and yet it kind of is.

Professor Sebastian growls, and we stop laughing. "Send word via mirror when you've reached Gilly's grandmother." The mirror goes dark.

ASSIGNMENT FOR: Professor Sebastian at Fairy Tale Reform School

SENT FROM: The middle of Enchantasia Sea during a sea squall

FIVE YEARS FROM NOW I WILL BE...

BY: Maxine Hockler

Forgive my handwriting, Professor! It's kind of hard to write when the ship is listing sideways and water keeps coming over the side of the ship. But we're fine! We got the ship up and running in less than a day! AG says not to worry about her. Ollie is a great navigator, while Jax seems to really like sailing. Kayla, Jocelyn, and Gilly have been great first mates, while AG and I huddle belowdecks, sort of green and queasy. I'm trying to distract myself by writing to you as we cross the sea during this storm to get to Gilly's grandmother. So back to the assignment...

My wishes are simple but true, and I don't need Darlene to grant them for me. Five years from now, I'd like to be teaching at Mother Goose Nursery and have my own oak tree near my parents with a view of the village. I'd also like to make enough money to start my own jewelry-making business so I can stop wanting other people's jewels and create my own pretty trinkets. But none of that really matters as much as my friends.

If Gilly, Jax, Kayla, Allison Grace, Ollie, Hayley, Jack, and even Jocelyn and I are still friends, then I know everything in my life will turn out exactly how it should. We keep each other in check. They keep me from wanting to pluck shiny jewels from people, and I keep them all from doing things that aren't right (like taking the Golden Goose back to Rumpelstiltskin. At least he only has one egg, not a goose that can make hundreds of them!). Things are a bit uncertain right now, and villains will always be looking for an opportunity, but when you have friends by your side, the future doesn't feel so grim.

GRADE: A! Nice work, Maxine. Extra points for being the first one done! Now tell your friends to get working on their projects as well.

—Professor S

Tricky Trickster

K ayla looks up from our map to the small island in front of us and frowns. "Are you sure this is the right place?"

"Aye! *X* marks the spot!" Ollie declares.

"Enough with the pirate talk already," Jocelyn says wearily.

She has a roll of parchment on her lap and has been writing all morning instead of helping with the ship tasks Blackbeard gave us. His penmanship isn't great, so it was hard to read his list, but I think it includes:

- Swab the deck (which basically means mop).
- Pick a powder monkey. (They have the tricky job of filling the cannons.)

- Be a good first mate! (Mates take care of the pulleys and anchors and also rig the sails from up high.)

"What be the trouble with me speak?" Ollie asks as he looks again through his spyglass at the island we're nearing.

"It's phony!" Jocelyn says. "You don't talk like that or wear an eye patch or smelly pirate clothes. You are a man of the sea, but be your own person, for fairy's sake. Save the rest for your paper for Professor Sebastian. 'I want to be a pirate captain,'" she says mockingly.

"What are you writing about?" Ollie narrows his eyes.

"How in five years you'll still be mean?" Jocelyn stands up, her right hand glowing with a fireball.

"Hey!" I snap. "We can't turn on one another now. We're in this together, aren't we?"

"Yes," Ollie and Jocelyn mumble.

"Speaking of papers, I already handed mine in and got an A!" Maxine beams with pride. The color is finally coming back to her grayish face after a full day of seasickness that kept her and AG belowdecks, where they both apparently wrote their papers and sent them off.

AG sighs. "Father says I can't have my grade till I come

home. I think he's trying to make sure I get back sooner rather than later."

"What did you write about?" I ask.

"I said I want to run a fairy pets organization that oversees the care of magical creatures." She shrugs. "Since I'm half-beast, who better to understand what each side needs?"

"I haven't even started my paper yet," Jax admits as he shinnies up a mast to adjust the sails again.

"Me either." Ollie bites his lip. "Maybe I can work on it when we get to shore. Has anyone seen my compass?" He pats his pockets and looks around. Kayla shrugs. "Oh! There it is!" He pulls it from inside Jocelyn's cape. Kayla, Maxine, and I applaud.

"Show-off." Jocelyn takes her parchment and heads to the upper deck as Ollie transforms a wooden sword into a bouquet of flowers and presents them to Kayla and Maxine.

"I forgot how much fun it is doing magic tricks," he says as he looks at the compass and steers the ship toward shore.

"Magic tricks are what got you thrown into FTRS," I remind him.

"For *stealing*, but magic can be fun too." Ollie looks at me. "I'm sure your grandma can show you plenty of fairy magic that you could learn to use. You're so lucky you've got fairy blood coursing through your veins!"

"I've never felt an ounce of fairy magic in me, so I doubt I have fairy skills." I lean on the railing and look at the tiny beach and deserted shoreline. I grab Ollie's spyglass and look harder. "Are you sure this is right? The island looks deserted. Why would my grandmother live here?"

"Maybe she's in hiding," Kayla guesses. "Fairies can be pretty reclusive and shy."

I hold up the small piece of parchment with the island's latitude and longitude and frown. "These are definitely the right coordinates. She sent them to my mother in case of emergency."

"Emergency? As in, don't visit unless the world is about to be cursed?" Kayla asks. "Interesting."

"Who would want to spend all their time alone?" I wonder. I can't imagine taking this voyage without my friends.

"We'll know the reason soon enough," Ollie says as Jax comes back down the mast and drops the anchor. "Ready the rowboat, we're going ashore!"

"Please let there be no krakens," Maxine pleads.

There aren't krakens. All we see on the uneventful rowboat ride over is a flock of seagulls that follow us then fly up and over the mountain as we near the beach. We pull the boat onto the sand and look around.

"No footprints, no sign of a home or anyone having been here." Jax looks through the spyglass. "Kayla?"

She flutters to the ground, and her wings retract and disappear. "I took a quick fly around the island. There are lots of trees, but not a single home or fairy hut. Of course, she could be shrunk down to fairy size, which would make finding a hut pretty difficult."

"She's got fairy blood, but we don't know what fairy traits she inherited," I say, looking around. There doesn't even appear to be a path leading off the beach. "I doubt she can shrink."

"Can you shrink?" Jocelyn pokes me in the ribs.

"Ouch! And no! Not that I know of. Poking isn't going to make it happen."

"Maybe you need to try," Kayla says brightly. "I wonder if you have wings and don't even know it. Then we could fly everywhere!"

"I could join you on Blue, and then we could all travel together!" Maxine smiles toothily, thinking of our friend the magic carpet.

"Yes, but Blue isn't here and Gilly's grandmother

supposedly is," Jocelyn snaps, looking up from her school paper, which she's carried to shore to continue working on. "Now where is she? *Pearl!* Isn't that her name? *Grandma Pearl! Where are you? Your granddaughter is here!*"

"Shh!" I nudge her. "She doesn't know I'm coming."

"Oh, fairies always sense when company is coming," Kayla confides. "She knows we're here."

"But does she *want* company?" Ollie pulls a sword out of his sheath, and we all gasp. "It's for protection. What if these here shores be booby-trapped?"

"Booby-trapped. Please!" Jocelyn starts walking up the beach, her black and purple cape dragging through the sand. The stars and moons on it seem to glint in the sunlight, casting shadows on the beach. I'm so busy staring at them that I don't realize Jocelyn is sinking till she's almost waist-deep in the sand. "Quicksand!" she shouts, and blasts fireball after fireball at the sand. "Someone take my paper! I don't want to start over."

Kayla flutters over and takes it from her hand. "Hang on. I'll pull you up."

"No!" Jocelyn insists. "Don't get any closer! You'll sink too!"

"Throw her a rope!" Ollie shouts.

"We don't have a rope!" Jax sprints to a nearby palm tree lying on its side on the beach. He grabs the dead branches and pulls the tree over to Jocelyn. "Grab on!" The rest of us help Jax pull her free.

Jocelyn pants. "Okay, so maybe there are booby traps."

"That means she's here," Kayla says, looking around. "Fairies have the best protection charms."

"Why didn't you mention that earlier?" Jocelyn snatches her scroll back from Kayla. "I need to finish this paper and send it off with a carrier pigeon before your grandma accidentally blows it up."

"What's the rush?" I ask.

Jocelyn gives me a look. "We're trying to stop a curse that could end the world, which means we're kind of busy. And I never leave my homework till the last second."

Huh. Who knew?

"Guys?" Maxine's voice warbles. "I think there is another booby trap headed our way."

I look up. Boulders as big as the boot my family lives in are rolling down the mountain toward the beach, and they're picking up speed.

"Run!" I shout.

Jocelyn and I dive into the water to avoid getting hit by the first boulder. The sky opens, and lightning bolts singe the palm tree we used to rescue Jocelyn. The wind whips up and rain pelts us with such intensity that it's hard to stay above water for too long.

"We need to find shelter!" I shout as we continue to tread water.

"We need to stay in the water. We can't get past the boulders," Jocelyn yells back. "They're coming too fast."

"Where are the others?" I can't even see the shore.

Suddenly I feel something peck my head.

"The seagulls are attacking!" Jocelyn shouts. She reaches her hand up to conjure a fireball, but it fizzles out in the rain and the wind. Jocelyn and I cling to each other as waves start to roll in, threatening to carry us out to sea.

One thing is clear. If this is Grandma Pearl's doing, she really doesn't want to meet me.

"Gilly! Jocelyn!"

I hear voices calling our names, but I can't tell where they're coming from.

"Gilly!"

Maxine, Kayla, and AG have rowed up behind us and

are suddenly pulling Jocelyn and me into her tiny boat. The small vessel can hardly stay upright in the heavy waves.

"Where are the oars?" Jocelyn cries.

"Gone!" AG replies.

"Where are Ollie and Jax?" I yell.

"We can't find them!" Maxine bellows.

The boat gets caught in a massive wave and races in to shore, straight into the path of a boulder. I'm waiting to be flattened like the Gingerbread Man when I see Ollie run out in front of the rock, grinning like a madman. It all happens so fast that I barely have time to scream. I close my eyes tight, not wanting to look. But when I open them a second later, Ollie is still here. He holds his ground, letting another boulder slam right into him. I watch as it rolls straight through my pirate-loving friend.

It's a mirage! The rain and birds are real though. I'm soaked and bruised.

"Come on! Jack figured out how to get past the booby traps!" Ollie shouts, enjoying the boulders flying straight through him. He grabs Kayla's hand and pulls her out of the boat. We scramble down the beach. Jax is waiting by the palm trees.

"Ready to get off the beach? Watch this!" He sticks out

his hand, and the air shimmers and wavers like a hallway at FTRS. For a split second, I see a different landscape behind it. Is that a cornfield? Jax pokes the air again, walks right through the trees, and disappears. Another mirage! We hurry after him, anxious to get out of the rain.

When I emerge on the other side, the sun is shining and the beach has given way to a massive cornfield. A basket of freshly picked corn sits untouched on the path, which tells me someone is definitely here. The path leads to a hill with a tiny stone house sitting atop it. Smoke plumes from the chimney, so someone definitely lives here.

"Fairy trickery at its finest," Kayla marvels. "Gilly, your grandmother is a genius. Let's go meet her!" She takes off down the path, fluttering toward the hillside. *Smack!* Kayla hits an invisible wall and falls to the ground.

"Maybe you just need a running start like this!" Jax races toward the same spot and gets flung backward. They both lie in a heap on the ground.

Now I've had it. "Grandma? That's enough! You've had your tricks. Now come out and face me like a grown woman!"

"Grown fairy," Maxine whispers.

Grandma Pearl still doesn't show up.

"Well, if she won't come to me, I'm going to her." I stomp over to the invisible wall and look for something—anything—that appears out of place. There's got to be a path around this blockade. There always is a way. My eyes search every speck of dirt and row of corn for an entrance. Suddenly, I spot a teal teakettle buried in the cornstalks. I reach out to grab it, and the whole barrier comes down.

A short, plump woman is standing on the other side. She has short, curly lilac hair and is wearing a long, flowy pink dress and a string of ivory pearls. She has a lilac purse on her shoulder as if she's heading to market. Whisper-thin purple wings flutter gently behind her back. Her silver wand is raised to attack, but she does not look surprised to see me.

"Took you long enough." She puts her wand safely back in her pocket. "I would have thought any granddaughter of mine would have realized the boulders were a mirage and a teakettle has no place in a corn maze right away."

"Hello, Grandma Pearl," I say, feeling suddenly nervous. "I'm your oldest granddaughter, Gilly. Thanks for nearly killing us on our quest to talk to you."

"Oh, you were perfectly fine! A little shock is good for the heart." She smiles at Jax and Ollie. "These fine young men were smart enough to realize the boulders were a ruse right away. Nice work, gentlemen."

"Thank you, Grandma Pearl." Ollie bows.

She looks me up and down and pulls her large purple purse higher on her shoulder. "You, however, Granddaughter, collapsed like Humpty Dumpty. Not sure what that says about your future and this curse, I'll tell you that."

"You know about the curse?" Kayla asks, her wings fluttering.

Grandma Pearl doesn't respond. She picks up her teakettle and turns toward the path to the cottage. "I suppose you're all hungry. You should eat before you leave the island." She pulls an hourglass out of her dress pocket. "You have an hour till you have to leave."

"An hour?" AG says. "Our clothes won't even be dry by then."

"An hour!" Grandma Pearl repeats. "That's more than enough time to eat and explain to my granddaughter why it's foolish to tangle with Rumpelstiltskin and Alva."

I'm stunned into silence. "You know Alva?"

Grandma Pearl looks back at me. Her violet eyes seem to come alive. "Of course, I know her. We were best friends."

CHAPTER 5

Pearls of Wisdom

Grandma Pearl's house is five times as large as it looks from the outside. And for someone who lives off the fairy-tale grid, she lays out a spread more lavish than I've seen at any royal court gathering. She even did a spell to dry us off and packed us a to-go bag of food and drinks for our journey home. Grandma Pearl has been a gracious hostess, but the sand in the hourglass keeps falling, and we're no closer to getting any information about Stiltskin and Alva.

My grandmother seems to want to talk to anyone *but* me. She even made me leave the magic mirror that links us to FTRS on her porch. ("I won't have people eavesdropping on me!")

Needless to say, I'm not hungry like the others.

"So are you going to talk to your grandmother about Alva or not?" Jocelyn is standing in the doorway between the kitchen and the dining room, watching my friends fill their plates and rave about my grandmother's chicken noodle soup. ("The cure for any seafaring aches!" she says proudly.)

"Yes," I say, but I don't move a muscle. Grandma Pearl is a bit intimidating.

"When? The hourglass is almost up, and we need information."

"I know that," I say, growing irritated. "I'll talk to her… soon."

Jocelyn scratches her chin. "I wonder if your grandmother is a villain, too, and this is actually a trap." She grins wickedly. "If so, I'd be impressed. Maybe you do have darkness running through you, after all."

I roll my eyes. "I do not. Don't get all excited."

"Who said I'm excited? You're the one with a grandma who is best friends with one of two villains trying to erase Enchantasia."

We both look at Grandma Pearl as she ladles more soup into everyone's bowls. She's chatting away happily, looking very much like a regular grandma. Nothing about her screams *villain*. Does it?

"All I'm saying is she seems to know a lot for someone who is hidden away on an island," Jocelyn adds. "And no one hides without a reason. It's your job to find out what it is."

I stare at a bowl of pudding on the kitchen counter that is being whisked on its own and sigh. "How? She doesn't seem interested in talking to me. She hasn't even asked about my father—her son—or about any of my brothers and sisters or whether any of us exhibit any fairy abilities. I don't even know if she knows my siblings exist!"

Jocelyn attempts to dip her finger in the pudding, and the whisk smacks her hand. "You have your opening right there. You can be charming when you want to be. Talk about her son and tell her something she doesn't know."

I stare at the hypnotic circling of the whisk, feeling unsure.

"Flash her that Cobbler smile, keep the sarcasm to a minimum, and I guarantee she'll be spoon-feeding you soup in no time." Her coal-like eyes stare right through me. "You can do this."

Did Jocelyn just pay me a compliment? I exhale slowly. "You're right. Thanks for the pep talk."

Jocelyn frowns. "You're not going to try to hug me now or anything, are you?"

I shrink back. "Absolutely not."

"Good."

"Good," I agree and turn to the dining room. "Can I have some soup?" I ask my grandmother.

Grandma Pearl's wings stop fluttering. "You're not even hungry. Why would you want soup?"

"I…" How does she know that? Everyone at the table looks at me.

"I have excellent hearing. All fairies do. I heard you talking to the Evil Queen's sister over there."

Jocelyn shrinks back into the shadows.

Grandma Pearl puts the pot of soup on the table. "Might as well get our talk over with. Come out on the porch. There is a nice view of the ocean out there."

She walks into the living room and opens double doors that lead to a balcony overlooking the water. I felt like we walked miles to her house, and yet her home seems to be right on the beach. Another fairy trick, I assume. Grandma takes a seat in a white rocker and motions to an older wooden one next to hers. I brush off some of the peeling paint and sit down.

"Your father made that for me when he was a boy. It's the only thing I took of his when I left twenty years ago."

I slide my hands along the wood, my fingers grazing the white and red hearts that are peeling away. "You were gone before I was even born."

"Yes." Grandma Pearl folds her hands in her lap and stares out at the sea as she rocks. "I left a lifetime ago. Haven't spoken to your father since, although I do check in from time to time in my own way. It's hard when I have to use traditional mail." She raises her eyebrows sharply. "That boy never wanted to explore his fairy heritage, so we can't communicate the way most fairies do."

"And what is that?" I ask, rocking my chair back and forth.

"A feeling. Sensation. Knowing someone is trying to reach us, I guess. We know when someone is in trouble, which is how I knew what you were up against." She give me another look. "That sister of yours—Anna, not Trixie—is trouble. Then again, you were trouble before you got sentenced to Fairy Tale Reform School too."

I stop rocking. "How do you know that?"

She narrows her eyes. "I'm not giving away all my secrets.

But I will say fairies have excellent senses and can also see the future. It's why so many of us are tasked with writing villains' stories—so we know them first and can try to stop them. Plus, your mother and I correspond by mini scroll," she adds hastily.

"You and Mother are in touch?" I'm gobsmacked. "I didn't think Mother kept any secrets."

"We all have secrets, child." Grandma sighs. "It's deciding who to trust them with that is the problem. I chose poorly. It's why I left and have kept my location secret from all but your mother for so long. Knowing me can bring a heap of trouble. Alva doesn't think too highly of me these days. Not that I think that highly of her either."

"You said you were best friends. How did that happen?"

Grandma Pearl smiles. "We met at Future Fairies boarding school. We were roommates actually. Best friends for years. She always had a temper, and I had a big mouth and said things I regretted a lot." She glances my way. "Just like you do."

I don't say anything.

"But for the most part, we were thick as a pair of thieves, which was uncommon for fairies. Our kind aren't the best at friendships, but Alva and I were always close." Her smile fades. "Until we weren't. When we were a bit older, I met your grandfather while she became obsessed with the royals in Enchantasia. Alva didn't like that they had the power to make decisions that affected all our lives. She felt the royals looked down on commoners."

My cheeks burn. Alva and I have more in common that I realized. I used to be the same way.

"Alva was particularly aggravated by the birth of baby Rose—felt her parents were making the child out to be some savior of the kingdom when she was just another child born with a silver spoon, so to speak. She and I were still friends, but I, too, grew tired of her constant railing against royals. When a bunch of us were invited to the baby's christening and she wasn't, well...things got ugly. She didn't want me attending, but I went anyway, and she showed up and cursed that baby before I could stop her. That's when I went after her. We raised our wands and had it out fairy style."

"A fairy showdown?" I say in awe. "That sounds intense."

Grandma Pearl side-eyes me. "Oh, it was. We both got pretty beat up. Alva cursed me to be unlucky in love, and I have been ever since. I lost your grandfather when your father was young and left your father when he was only a child himself. Alva's curse prevented me from being a good mother, I'm ashamed to say. Your mother is the one who hunted me down and tried to reconcile the two of us, but what's done is done. All I really care about these days is myself."

"I used to be like that," I admit. "I think about my friends in the other room and Fairy Tale Reform School, how it's changed me and all it could do for Anna if I could get her there. But I'm starting to see—"

"The world is a lot bigger than just you and me, and life isn't worth living if you don't use your powers to help those around you," Grandma Pearl finishes.

"Yes," I realize. Grandma Pearl seemed to take the words right out of my head.

A small smile plays on her lips. "It's good to see Alva's curse will die with me." Her expression changes. "But still. Your father wouldn't want you here, and he certainly wouldn't want you to have a relationship with me."

So that's why Grandma Pearl seems so unfriendly. Alva cursed her ability to love. "What curse did you put on her?"

Grandma Pearl beams. "I was clever—like you, I suppose. I didn't choose something obvious. For all I know, Alva has never even realized my curse worked. I cursed her with shortsightedness."

"How?" I wonder in awe.

"She's impulsive! Doesn't think things through. With Rose, she didn't fully flesh out her curse. That's what gave the sleeping princess the ability to wake. When she fought you all at school, she morphed into a dragon without realizing her dragon weaknesses. With Rumpelstiltskin, she foolishly fell in love, knowing she could never really commit to anyone but herself. She's selfish, but he still became obsessed with her. That's *his* greatest weakness." She points at me. "*Remember what I am telling you.* It *might* help you in your final battle with Alva. I'm afraid there will be one. I have seen it clear as day." She looks at me curiously. "Do you get premonitions yet?"

"No. I haven't shown any sort of fairy skills, to be honest."

She purses her lips. "Not true. You've opened a villain book. I've seen that too."

"You have?" I stand up. "But how?"

She waves her hand away. "No time to explain. The point is, you have fairy traits running through you. I can feel it. You just need to focus and listen to your inner voice if you want to survive that final battle."

I stop her chair from rocking and look at her. "You seem to know them better than anyone. Come back with me and help us stop them."

"No." Grandma removes my hands from her chair and starts to rock again. "I already fought her once. I won't do it again." She looks at me. "My fairy skills have grown weak with age. Yours will become stronger over time. You just need to concentrate."

"I've already got enough to think about," I complain. "Alva and Stiltskin are creating a curse that will rewrite time!"

"Embracing your fairy side is important! You hear me? Our bloodline is strong. It doesn't diminish with new generations. Your father always suppressed his fairy abilities, which is why he never told you about our heritage. He was angry at me, and it seemed easier to forget. But for you, being a fairy is an asset. You're nimble—that's a fairy trait; you're a trickster—also a fairy trait; and clever—another fairy trait. You probably can't fly, but it's overrated, and talking to animals is something many full-fledged fairies can't even manage. You can learn clairvoyance, illumination, and possibly even invisibility, but it all takes time." She taps her chin. "If you're going to fight Alva and win, you must concentrate on strengthening the skills you already have inside you."

"But I only have a few days!" I say, exasperated. "There is a Fire Moon coming, and that's when the curse will be cast!"

Grandma Pearl's eyes widen. "A Fire Moon? Oh, that's not good." She gets out of her chair and walks to the balcony railing. "Not good at all. Last time there was one of those, well, there's no use wasting time telling you." She points to me again. "You need to find your inner fairy! It's the only way you'll be able to be part of a quorum to stop her."

"A what?"

"Quorum. Since fairies are loners, getting a group of them together to fight for the same cause is rare. But if you could get six fairies to join you, you could beat her. You just have to all want the same thing and have the best of intentions. We couldn't get a quorum together for young Rose, obviously."

"I know several fairies," I say brightly.

"Do you know six who show fairy abilities? Your father and your siblings don't count if they don't show any skills."

I frown. "No."

"You're not a full-blooded fairy, so your fairy skills must be perfect to ensure it will work. You can't let Anna distract you. I'm not even sure that one can be saved." She wags a finger at me. "Continuing to try to save her has been your biggest downfall." I open my mouth to protest. "People can change, but only if they really want to."

Professor Wolfington once told me the same thing.

"Stop trying to control the things you can't control and focus on the things you can. You have it in you to fight this darkness. You just have to concentrate! Don't be sloppy or blinded by your emotions."

"But I can't help it," I say desperately. "I love Anna. I love my friends and my school. I want to help them."

"Oh child. That's your problem." Grandma Pearl shakes her head. "Thanks to Alva, I don't know what love is like. Sure, her curse has faded somewhat over time, but not enough for me to crave the company of others. I'm happy on my own. Must be hard caring about others so much. Still, you must decide what's more important: Saving Anna or the whole of Enchantasia?"

"Enchantasia," I whisper, but I feel ill at the thought of abandoning Anna.

"Good girl." Grandma Pearl slips something into my hand. It's a beaded necklace with a red crystal vial hanging from it. "Here. This is a protective charm. It wards off Alva. I've had it on for years, but you need it more than I do now. It won't help you avoid her forever, but it will help you stay cloaked for the most part."

"But now you won't be protected," I protest.

She shrugs. "What's the old bat going to do to me at this point? She took away my chance to love, but I still got to meet you, didn't I?" She smiles. "So maybe love isn't completely out of my life, after all."

Now I am all choked up. "Grandma…"

"Hush! No tears. You know now what you need to do—hone your fairy skills and be ready to fight once your friends find the harp. Keep it safe! You don't have much time to do all this, but I know you're up for the challenge." She looks at the hourglass. The last of the sand is about to fall. "Seek help in your friends. Don't make the mistake I made and shut yourself away from the world, child."

"I promise." Despite my better judgment, I reach out and hug her. She doesn't stop me.

I hear a loud pop, and a bell begins to chime. The sound is earsplitting. Grandma Pearl breaks away.

Maxine comes running. "What's going on?"

Grandma Pearl pulls out her wand. "Your time is up. I've removed my protection charm and given it to you. She knows where I am…and that you're here."

There is a high-pitched screeching sound, and I look to the sky. In the distance, I see a flock of winged creatures headed our way. There are dozens of them.

"Gargoyles," Grandma Pearl says hollowly. "Such wretched minions. I always told Alva she could do better, but she never listened."

"We don't have any radishes!" Kayla cries. "What will we do?"

"Grandma Pearl, have you grown any radishes on the island?" Ollie pulls at her sleeves. "They're the only things we know of that fight beasties."

"Oh, child, they're afraid of a lot more than radishes. But there's no time to explain." Grandma Pearl pulls the group of us together. "I'm more than equipped to handle a few foul-breathed foes. But they can't find you." She looks me straight in the eye as she waves her wand and forms a protective bubble around us. "This bubble will take you somewhere safe. Tell your pirate friend I'm sorry about his ship. I will hold them off."

"But—" There's still so much I want to say and ask.

And maybe, just maybe, get another hug.

Grandma Pearl lifts her chin. "No buts. We're out of time."

Jocelyn's hands press against the bubble. "We need to get back to Fairy Tale Reform School. Can you get us there?"

Grandma Pearl bites her lip. "I think I know the coordinates. Now pipe down. I need to concentrate!" She picks up her bag, slides it onto her arm, and fluffs her purple hair. Her wings begin to flutter as she waves her wand and the bubble we're in begins to shimmer. I touch the bubble. She presses her palm against it from the other side just as the first gargoyle lands on her balcony. Grandma Pearl smiles. "Make me proud, Granddaughter."

And with a wave of her wand, we disappear.

CHAPTER 6

Giant-Sized Problems

We are spinning so fast that the world and the people around me are a complete blur. I feel like we are being stretched like taffy, and there's a whizzing sound in my ears growing so loud that I can't hear my own screaming. Just when I think I can't stand it a moment longer, the bubble slows down and begins to deflate before dropping softly onto the ground.

It bursts, and we all tumble out.

Traveling by bubble is a lot different than traveling by magic bean.

Ollie promptly loses his lunch. "What in the name of Grimm did she just do to us?"

"Saved our necks." Jax holds his head in his hands as he

slowly sits up. "I think. I'll know once the world stops spinning. Are we back at school?"

"I think so. Is everyone all right?" Words feel strange on my lips, and I'm shivering. I look around, trying to get my bearings. These trees don't look familiar and the ground is really squishy, like there's been a lot of rain. We seem to be on a hill.

Kayla springs right up. "That was incredible! Your grandmother could be fairy queen. I don't know any fairies that can travel by bubble! That's an upper-level skill most of us can't do. Once, my mother formed a bubble, but it only lasted a second before it burst. Your grandmother used it to send us all the way across the ocean and the kingdom to…school?" She frowns. "This doesn't look like school grounds."

Maxine bites her lip. "I don't think we're home. This terrain feels odd." Maxine bounces up and down and almost falls. "Careful! The ground is really uneven."

"I think her magic might be wonky," Jocelyn says. "Who knows if we're even in the Hollow Woods right now." Jocelyn stands up, readjusts her cloak, and looks around.

"Why would it be wonky?" I know I just met my grandmother, but I feel a tad protective of her. "We told her where we needed to go."

"Yes, but she hasn't been back in Enchantasia in years," Jocelyn reminds me. "What if she had the coordinates wrong? We could be in any forest from here to Oz or Avalon."

"Quick!" Kayla says. "Try using your untapped fairy skills to figure out where we are."

"How do I do that?" I ask skeptically.

"I don't know." Kayla's wings pop out and flutter madly. "Clairvoyance isn't one of my things, but it is your grand-mother's, so you should have it. Concentrate! Can you see the future? Where are we?" Everyone looks at me hopefully.

I close my eyes, exhale long and slow, and think. *Where are we?* I have no clue. All I see is blackness, which makes sense because my eyes are closed. *Okay, Gilly. Try again. Think of the future? We are... We are...* "I have no clue where we are." Kayla sighs. I spin around, looking for a normal sign we're exactly where we should be, but I don't see the turrets of Fairy Tale Reform School in the distance. I kick the dirt, frustrated. "This doesn't look like school. What if Jocelyn is right, and we're totally in another kingdom? We have to get back before the Fire Moon."

"Maybe we should spread out and try to find a way out of this forest so we can get a better idea of where we are." Jax tries to stay upright but keeps tripping. It almost feels as if the hill just got steeper.

Ollie pulls out his sword. "Although if this is the Hollow Woods, we don't want to go *too* far alone."

"Oh my gnome." AG clutches her stomach. Her uniform is grass-stained and covered in tiny soap bubbles. "My parents forbid me from ever setting foot in the Hollow Woods. Or any wood, really. They don't even like hollow trees." She starts to hyperventilate.

"Don't worry," I stumble, feeling unsteady on my feet. "If it's the Hollow Woods, we've been here before."

"I've been here more times than you," Jocelyn says and loses her balance.

"What difference does it make how many times you or I have been here?" I pick up my quiver-and-arrow pack and place it on my shoulder again. "The Hollow Woods is not dangerous...if you know how to navigate it. And we do."

"We did it *once*," Jax reminds me.

"We're practically experts!" I insist. I don't add how lost we got in here last time or how we faced down a Bandersnatch. Sometimes it's better not to share every detail. "Let's get going. We need to move fast and get back to school."

"We might not be anywhere near school!" Jocelyn says again.

Kayla touches her neck. "Yeah, Gilly, my neck is prickly like something is wrong. Do you feel that too?" she asks hopefully. "Any sensation at all?"

I shake my head. "Nope." Kayla looks disappointed.

"Everyone stop talking right now!" AG shouts, her breath coming fast. Her eyes are wild. "Kayla is right! Something is very wrong here."

We all look at her. AG never yells at anyone. She must be really worked up. Traveling by bubble will do that to a person.

"I don't care if you're practically royalty," Jocelyn snaps. "No one talks to me like that."

"AG's right. There is something strange about this place," Maxine backs up a few paces and disappears. I hear her scream.

"Maxine!" Kayla flutters over and disappears over the other side of the hill. I didn't realize it was that steep.

"This isn't a hill!" AG says, and I watch as hair starts to sprout on the back of her hands and her mouth starts to elongate. "My senses are telling me this mound is alive."

The whole hill starts to rumble. "Don't move! You'll wake the... *Awhoo!*" AG falls to all fours, and her yellow dress begins ripping as her limbs grow. (She's going to be so upset. That party dress is her favorite.) Claws grow out of her hands and feet, and her nose becomes a snout. She sniffs the air, gives another howl, and disappears over the other side of the hill.

Wake the... What in the name of fairies does AG mean?

I hear a loud roar, and I know immediately what my non-existent fairy skills have blatantly missed. "Everyone follow AG! This isn't a hill, it's a giant!"

I start running and get tossed backward as a giant rises from its slumber. As it stands up, we all go sliding down its backside. I see the ground coming closer at alarming speed and can do nothing to stop it. Ollie tumbles past me along with Jocelyn, while Jax shoots downward like a silver bullet. At the last second, I see Jax's rope hook onto the giant's pants. He comes to a jarring stop as he hangs from the giant's waistband.

"Catch it!" I hear Jax cry.

I scramble to grab the rope, straining to hold it and not fall. Jax and I hang on for dear life as the giant begins to move and emits a loud roar. *Please don't squish my friends. Please don't squish my friends.*

Whoosh! I see the giant's large hand reach down and try to grab me and Jax. We swing away just in time. *Whoosh!* His other hand reaches for us. We kick off on the rope again, swinging out of reach. This isn't good either. We're directly in the giant's path. If he grabs our rope and pulls us upward, we're going to be his lunch. Somewhere in the distance, I hear a wolf howl. Then I see a fireball come rocketing straight toward us. It comes dangerously close to singeing my thigh. The giant roars again, lifting one leg and getting thrown off balance.

"We need to get down!" Jax shouts to me. "On the count of three, we swing and I cut the rope. One…"

"Cut the rope?" We must be forty feet off the ground.

"Two!"

"Jax, we're too high up!"

Whoosh! The giant's hand reaches for us again.

"Three!" Jax cuts the line, and we start to free-fall. I bash into the giant's thigh, then hit his muddy knee as I continue to tumble downward. The ground is coming dangerously close when I feel Kayla's hands on me.

"Gotcha both!" she says, holding one of us in each of her hands. She starts to glide away, and a shadow crosses her face.

"Watch out!" I cry as the giant's hand knocks into us. The three of us spin off course, landing in a bush where the others are hiding.

"Are you all right?" Maxine helps us up. AG licks my hand. "We thought you were goners."

The giant roars in frustration. Then I hear another roar in the distance. And another. This giant is not alone, and unlike the giants in Cloud City, forest giants are not so friendly. Their size alone is scary enough, but they also hate intruders and aren't usually willing to listen to reason.

Jocelyn throws her hands up. "Great! Now we've woken a tribe of sleeping giants. We don't have time to fight them off. We have to get to FTRS." She conjures a fireball. "Maybe if I start a small fire, they'll back away."

Maxine smacks her hand away. "*No!* You can't start a fire in a forest! You'll burn the whole place down. We just have to talk to them sensibly and say, 'Giants, we're a bit busy right now, trying to save Enchantasia and all, and it would be wonderful if we could tango another day." She grins. "Do you think that will work?"

"No," we collectively reply.

The sound of stomping gets closer, the ground rattling beneath our feet. It sounds like an army of giants is headed our way.

I grab an arrow from my quiver and place it in the bow at the nocking point. I pull back and Maxine smacks my hand, ruining my aim.

"What are you doing? You can't hurt a giant! Think of Erp. And Jack. We promised Jack we'd never hurt another giant."

Ever since Jack learned the giants he met at the top of the beanstalk weren't the villains he made them out to be, he's been trying to change the kingdom's views of them. He even has weekly meet and greets with Erp, a giant who helped us in Cloud City. Most kids are still too terrified to go near him. When you're friends with someone as tall as a house, it can be intimidating.

"But giants native to the woods are a lot different from ones who were raised at the top of a beanstalk," Jax reminds her.

"It doesn't matter! Giants are giants." Maxine sets her lip. "We're not hurting them."

"Even though this group is headed our way to eat us?"

Ollie points to a large tree in their path. The giants flick it, and it topples as easily as if they were brushing lint off their boots.

"Well, how are we going to get away from them without fireballs or arrows?" I ask in exasperation. "We can't hide out here forever! Stiltskin could already be on his way to school."

Jocelyn conjures up another fireball. "I'm firing one."

"No!" Maxine jumps in front of Jocelyn's hand. "It's not right!"

The ground shakes even harder and knocks Maxine to the ground. Kayla and Ollie hold on to each other.

"Give me a boost into this redwood tree so I can get a better look at what we're up against," I tell Jax. He makes a hold for my boot so I can hoist myself up.

"You're going to fall," Kayla warns me, her wings fluttering wildly. "Try focusing on wings, and maybe yours will appear!"

I'm not even going to attempt that one. Instead, I focus on my footholds. The higher I go, the better the view. Halfway up the redwood, I see the giants moving in a slow pack. "There's five or six of them," I yell down to the others. "Way more than we've faced in the past. We need an escape plan if we can't fight them." I look left and see a river, but we've got no flotation devices. I look right and see more trees…and more giants moving in our direction. I look behind me, and it's more bad news. More giants, more trees.

I don't see FTRS anywhere.

Grandma Pearl, if we meet again, we need to work on your sense of direction.

Whiz!

Something shoots past me, almost slicing off my nose. What was that? A butterfly? Hummingbird? Baby dragon?

Whiz! Whiz! Whiz!

I cling to my tree branch as something fast, light, and bright heads straight for me. I duck just in time and see an arrow lodge in the branch inches above my head. An almost translucent rope is hanging from it. Humpty Dumpty, what is that?

Whiz!

Something much larger than an arrow is barreling down the line, coming straight for me. I pull myself up to the next-highest perch just in time to see someone slide down the rope and land on my branch. An older boy with fair hair and bright-blue eyes flashes me a killer smile. He's wearing a leather vest with matching leather boots, and his outfit blends in expertly with the surrounding forest. On his back, he carries a bow and a quiver of arrows.

He grins. "Aha! So it is you, Gillian Cobbler! She was right, after all."

CHAPTER 7

Hoodwinked

Who is this boy?

"I'm sorry," I say. "Do I know you?"

He cocks his head. "Well, you certainly should."

Whiz!

A girl comes flying into the boy and stops short of knocking him off the branch. She pulls off her hood and smiles at me. "Gilly! Am I glad to see you!"

"Red?" Red Riding Hood is here? That means we're still in Enchantasia, and this has to be the Hollow Woods! Thank the fairies. "How did you find me?" I ask. "And who is this guy?"

Red looks at him, waiting for him to tell me.

The boy sighs. "You'd think everyone would know Robin Hood by now."

"*The* Robin Hood?" Even I'm impressed. He's wanted everywhere! He just got in trouble for helping some expelled Royal Academy kids escape Headmistress Olivina's clutches—before she was exposed for her villainy and disappeared without a trace, that is.

He bows. "At your service, young hero."

Red rolls her eyes. "Robin, stop charming and start working. We don't have the time." She takes an arrow from her own quiver and fires it into the unknown. I watch the glowing string attached to it keep going and going, wondering where it's headed. The rope seems to be some sort of travel system the outlaws have rigged.

"Right!" Robin looks up and down. "Where is everyone else? We should be on our way. No time to waste."

"They're down below."

A loud roar almost sends me tumbling out of the tree.

"Ah, I see. Let me give them a hand up here while you both keep the giants busy." Robin swings down and out of sight as Red fires another arrow in the giants' direction. I can see the giants closely now. They're only a few trees away.

"Um, Red?" I say delicately. "Maxine doesn't want us hurting the giants."

"These giants aren't like the ones you faced in Cloud City," Red says as the ground shakes.

"I know, but Maxine feels everyone deserves a second chance and…"

Screech!

I stop talking. Red and I look at each other.

Gargoyles?

A huge flock of them, bigger than the group at Grandma Pearl's, are flying over the treetops.

"It can't be!" I complain. "We just saw them across the ocean! They couldn't have made it here yet." How'd they find us? I'm wearing Grandma Pearl's protective necklace! I assumed it hid me from gargoyles and Alva, but maybe it's just her? I don't understand. Unless… Did Stiltskin make a wish to find my location?

"Who cares how they got here?" Red yells. "You've got to go!" We both duck as a gargoyle narrowly misses grabbing us.

"Me? You mean all of us, right?"

Red places one of her arrows in my hand. I notice it glows. "No time to wait. Take this and hold on tight."

"To an arrow? How does this…"

"Don't ask questions!" Red fires an arrow that's not glowing at the beasties. "When I let go, hang on."

"To the arrows?" I look down and see Robin leading the others up the tree. The screeching and roars continue to get louder.

"Yes." Red grows frustrated. "You trust me, right?" She takes my hand and closes it over the arrow as another gargoyle bears down on us.

"Yes, but…"

"Good." Red closes my hand around the arrow. "Hold on!"

"Hold on to wha—*ahh!*" As soon as my fingers close around the arrow, it takes off, whizzing through the forest at a speed even faster than the bubble. I can't see my feet, the ground, or the arrow's target, but I hold on tight because I don't have a safety net. The arrow ducks and weaves between trees, through a waterfall, and over a mountainside. Suddenly, I see something huge coming right at me. The arrow doesn't stop. It hits a large hand and bounces off, sending me flying. More giants! The hand closes around me. I struggle to get out of its grasp.

"Gilly! Stop! It's us!"

I stop pushing on the fingertips and look up. My friend Jack, who is famous for climbing beanstalks, is sitting on the giant's shoulder. This giant has red hair that stands straight up on his head. He sees me and smiles toothily. "Jack? Erp?" The giant mumbles something I don't understand. "What are you doing here? And where are we?"

"On the other side of the Hollow Woods near the village," Jack explains. I notice he's wearing his FTRS school uniform. The giant is wearing a bright-blue shirt that looks like the uniform as well. "Erp and I are on special assignment from Headmistress Flora and Professor Wolfington." He winces. "It's actually detention, but I prefer this to dance class with Madame Cleo. We are supposed to patrol the borders and report anything we see that's suspicious. We're also attempting to convince some giants to join our forces and help stop Rumpelstiltskin. But I didn't know you were here or I would have... *Heads up!*"

Erp shoots me high into the air and reaches down to grab the rest of my friends, who have all hitched a ride on one extra-long arrow. They land in Erp's arms right before I fall back down into his hand as well.

"That was amazing!" Ollie says as he tumbles out of Erp's

grasp and climbs up his arm. "We should only travel by magic arrow now!"

Erp places us all gently on the ground. Kayla is crying.

"We tried to tell Kayla you were just ahead of us, but she was panicked," Jocelyn explains.

"I can't help it"—Kayla's eyes well with tears—"I was so worried when you disappeared. It's like the gargoyles have you on lock. I thought they caught your arrow. Why are they after you?"

"I don't know," I admit, my eyes on the sky, barely visible above the trees.

"Well, we're safe and I can't believe we're meeting *the* Robin Hood!" Maxine says, drool dribbling down her chin as she stares at Robin. "You're a legend!"

He kisses her ogre hand. "Thanks, little lady. I'm not sure about being a *legend*, but I do pride myself on doing good for others and—"

Red clears her throat. "You do this every time we meet someone new!"

"What?" Robin protests, his big eyes wide and innocent.

"Talk about yourself and try to charm the ladies!" Red complains.

Maxine clutches her heart. "Robin Hood is trying to charm *me*?" She looks like she may pass out. Great. And I don't think any of us have smelling salts.

"I do not," Robin says, blushing slightly.

"Do too!" Red counters. "And right now we have more important things going on, like making sure we get Gilly back to that school."

"You mean all of us, right?" I ask, and Robin looks at Red again. "Okay, I'm not going anywhere till you tell me what's going on! What's with the sudden obsession with me staying safe?"

Red places a hand on my shoulder. "I think you should check your mirror."

My mirror. Is it even still here? I reach down to my sheath and find the mirror safely tucked away. The wooden handle is cracked, but it's still intact. The mirror is glowing a pulsing purple.

"We just got the alert ourselves a short while ago," Robin says quietly. "It's how we knew you were here."

"I don't understand," I tell Red.

"Just look at the mirror," she says tentatively.

"Hello?" I say to my reflection.

Angelina and Harlow shimmer into view, along with Flora. "Gilly! Thank goodness. Get back to this school immediately!"

"Stilstkin has made his first wish," Harlow says grimly. "And he used it on you."

I knew it! "How? Darlene said she would try hard not to let him cast any evil wishes."

"She didn't." Flora sighs. "Instead, he asked for the ability to track your location. It's how he knew you were in the woods. You need to get back here where we can cloak you. Harlow is working on a spell."

Clever move. "But why is he tracking me?" I want to know and Harlow and Flora look at each other.

"We aren't sure," Angelina says, "but I know you are a part of his story. I already told you that I see the Cobblers tied up in this curse, but now… When I was writing in his villain book today, I saw you standing beside him while the curse was cast."

"Me," I whisper. I feel a deep pit forming in my stomach. It's not possible. "I would never help him!"

"We know," Flora interrupts. "But for all our sake, you need to get back to FTRS right away so we can keep you safe. The Fire Moon is two days away."

"Can't you just shoot one of those arrow things and send us on our way?" Jax asks Robin, who is leaning against a tree listening.

"No can do. Flora 'ol girl says it isn't safe to let you go straight to the school gates."

"We're being watched," Flora tells us. "You'll have to use an underground entrance."

"We have those?" I ask.

"One or two," Flora says. "The one I'm thinking of has never been used. It was built in case of emergency, and this is definitely an emergency. It's in the basement of Pinocchio's Puppet Theatre."

"Wow, that would have been cool to know last year when I was craving pattycakes," Ollie says.

"*Ollie*," Harlow warns.

"I'm not saying I'll use it when we're back at school, but…" Ollie trails off.

"We'll let Pinocchio know you're coming," Flora says, "but be careful. Don't talk to too many people at the theater. Stay undercover and get back here fast."

I hesitate. I'd give anything to stop at my family boot and warn everyone to be on the lookout for Stiltskin, but there is no time. I'll just have to get a Pegasus Post off right away. Then I'll write that paper for Professor Sebastian. Priorities.

"We can't let the gargoyles find you," Angelina adds.

"We don't even have anything to fight them with," Ollie tells them, looking over my shoulder. "Every beastie knows that. The radish shortage makes it impossible."

"Radish and strawberry," I remind him.

"Radish shortage?" Robin laughs uncontrollably. Red hits him. "Sorry. It's just so amusing."

"What is, prince of thieves?" Jocelyn asks him.

"The radish shortage!" Robin can't stop chuckling. "Red and I caused it."

"You did?" Jax asks in surprise.

Red's cheeks color. "Not on purpose. Once we realized Stiltskin was back with Alva, and he was trying to destroy the radish crops to keep people from defending themselves against the gargoyles, we started hoarding them."

"We hid every radish there was left in the kingdom and have been growing a secret stash," Robin says proudly. "We've got them hidden all over the forest." He walks over to what appears to be a dead tree, yanks on what looks like a weed, and the hollow tree opens up like a trunk. There is a staircase inside it. Robin hurries down the stairs, then comes back a few seconds later with several small sacks. "Here you go!" My friends cheer.

"This is the first bit of good news we've had in a while," Maxine says, sounding emotional as Robin hands each of us a sack of radishes.

"Would have been nice if one of you could have sent word to us," Harlow says darkly.

"Sorry, Harlow," Red says. "We were trying to be discreet."

"But why did you take the strawberries too?" Jax asks. "Who do they ward off?"

"No one!" Robin grins. "I just love strawberries. Plus, it was funny to see people panic and wonder."

Red shakes her head. "He could use time at Fairy Tale Reform School, I think. But that will have to wait. You need to get going!"

"Wait! There's one more thing," Jack says. "A few friends of yours were depressed being at FTRS without you, so Headmistress Flora let us borrow them. Erp?"

Erp puts a hand in his giant shirt pocket and pulls out a tiny duck and something even smaller—a mouse.

"Peaches!" Maxine cries when she sees her magical fairy pet.

Erp drops the duck into her hand. Wilson, my fairy pet mouse, is sitting on Peaches's back. I pluck him off. He squeaks angrily at me.

"I know. I know! I'm sorry!" I say as Wilson continues to squeak. "I didn't mean to leave you behind, but you told me you got seasick the one time you were on a boat, so I thought it was safer for you to stay back at school." Even angrier squeaking comes out of his tiny mouth. "No, I won't leave you again. I swear! We're partners."

"Us too, Peaches," says Maxine, squeezing the duck in a hug. She lets go, and the duck looks me up and down. Then it pulls the mirror out of my hand and swallows it.

"No!" we all shout as we watch the long mirror disappear.

"Peaches!" Maxine scolds. "We need that! You give it back. Just the way it was! This instant!"

Peaches starts to cough, then gag, then shoots the mirror out of her mouth again. It looks slightly different.

"What just happened?" I hear Harlow yelling. "Where was that foul place?"

"Uh…we just dropped you," Ollie says, looking grossed out.

"Hey! Why is the mirror smaller?" I whisper, turning it over in my hands. I'm trying not to gag over the duck saliva. I wipe it on my uniform skirt.

Maxine shrugs. "I don't know. Sometimes when Peaches swallows things, they shrink."

"Swallows? At least it still works. Don't be so careless!" Harlow says with a sigh. "Now get that duck and yourselves to the passageway. Pronto."

"Sister?" Jocelyn pipes up. "Tell Professor Sebastian my homework scroll is on the way." She smiles at us smugly. "I finished it when we were waiting to take the arrow. A good writer doesn't need the perfect writing spot to work."

Show-off.

I hear Peaches gagging again. Up comes a small glass heel.

"Hey!" Jax grabs it and wipes it off with his shirt. "I remember that. Didn't Jocelyn bewitch this heel so she could talk to us?"

"Yes," Jocelyn says. "And look how well you took care of it."

"Peaches must have known we needed it and kept it just in case." Maxine beams at her duck proudly.

Jax slips it in his back pocket. "Maybe we can use it to communicate with others too. When we need to."

Screech!

The gargoyles are back.

Red pulls me in for a hug. "Go. We'll hold them off." She pulls back and looks at me. "Focus on stopping this curse, and forget about what part you play in his story. That's just baggage you don't need to carry. You hear?"

I nod. We don't get to spend much time together, but Red gets me in a way I sometimes don't even get myself.

She smiles. "This kingdom always thinks it knows exactly how a story will end, but it forgets something very important every time."

"What's that?" I ask as I hear more screeching. The others gather up their radishes and talk to Robin about directions.

Red taps my forehead. "Free will. You decide. Remember that."

I smile. "I will."

She throws a rope up and pulls it tight on a branch. Then she hoists herself up as Erp and Jack prepare to ride off again.

Robin shoots an arrow into the dark tree line, looks back at Maxine, and winks. "It was a pleasure meeting you, little lady." She giggles.

In the distance we hear Red. "*Robin!* Come on!"

He turns to me and bows, then reaches up to grab his rope. He zips off, but I can still hear him. "Till we meet again, Gilly Cobbler!"

ASSIGNMENT FOR: Professor Sebastian at Fairy Tale Reform School

SENT FROM: Somewhere in the Hollow Woods while under attack by giants (Not that I'm nervous or anything)

FIVE YEARS FROM NOW I WILL BE...

BY: Jocelyn (No last name needed as my sister is the Evil Queen)

Let's just get the honesty out of the way at the beginning of this essay, shall we?

I have no clue where I'll be in five years.

Anyone who tells you otherwise is yanking your beast beard. (No offense.)

Listen, when you're raised by one of the

greatest villains Enchantasia has ever seen, you
don't spend too much time worrying about the
future. You live for today. Villains are constantly under attack, so they have no clue whether they'll
see another sunrise. (Sure, my sister is confident,
but fears like this kept me up at night in my dungeon bedroom before we moved to FTRS.)

If I want something, I make it happen. I don't
wait for tomorrow because there may not be one.
Look at what's going on in Enchantasia. By the
time you get this, a curse could have wiped out
most of the kingdom. Villains may survive, but who
can really say? My point is, I don't look ahead.
Right now, all I want to do is keep this crew I'm
somehow a part of from losing their heads. So
yeah, I guess I do care about something—them.
Sometimes. Other times they're quite irritating.
And, of course, I do feel deeply for my sister who
raised me.

But since I know you're not going to be happy
unless I say I'm going to do something specific, I
will tell you one small idea I have.

Don't tell anyone about it, okay? It might ruin my rep.

I think—maybe—I might be good at creating countercurses. I've always been great in potions, not surprisingly, and I can read the most high-level spell books there are, not to brag. Maybe Red could use some of my potions in her shoppe. Fiddlesticks, I'll have my own shoppe next door, and then one day I'll buy out that red-cape-loving girl's shoppe too!

But again, that's if we're all here long enough to make it happen.

GRADE: B for honesty, which is refreshing from the sister of a (former) villain. I hope you will run a potion shop someday—and use your quick wit and skills for GOOD. —Professor S

CHAPTER 8

Counting Sheep

E veryone stay alert," I say as we cut through some bushes and emerge on a street full of boots and teakettle homes in Enchantasia Village. "We have no idea how long Red and Robin can hold off the beasties."

"Robin," Maxine says his name and starts giggling. Peaches quacks at her as she waddles along the path beside us. Maxine blushes. "I do not! He's just lovely, that's all." Peaches quacks again. "No, I don't want you to go back and snatch one of his arrows as a souvenir. Gilly's right. We need to stay together."

Jocelyn looks around warily. "Does anyone know what time it is?"

Jax pulls out his tricked-out pocket watch, which has

gotten us out of a scrape once or twice before. I haven't seen him carry it in a long time. "Around three o'clock. Why?"

Jocelyn looks around warily. "Street is pretty empty for the middle of the afternoon."

There are bikes and toys strewn on front lawns as if the kids were called in to dinner and left everything where it was. We walk by a Hot Tea for Sale stand and the teakettle is steaming, which means the stand's owners just made it. They couldn't have gone far.

"Maybe everyone is just getting out of school," AG suggests.

I pull an arrow out of my quiver and prepare to nock it. "Or we're about to be attacked."

"If we were going to be attacked, I think we'd know," Ollie said. "The beasties have been in clear view all along. They're not even trying to hide."

"Let's just move quickly," I say, hurrying down the street as Wilson pokes his pink nose out of my uniform pocket and squeaks in agreement. "We need to get to Pinocchio's Puppet Theatre unseen in case anyone here is looking for us."

"Don't think that's going to be a problem," Jocelyn says as we turn onto another empty street. "Is it a holiday or something?"

"Not that I know of." Jax frowns. "Let's see what's going on in the village square."

"I thought we were going to try to stick to the side streets." I turn onto another block of boot homes that look identical to the one I grew up in. "I know a lot of shortcuts."

I wasn't going to mention this out loud, but if we keep heading down Humpty Dumpty Court and then cut through the backyard of the old woman who lives in a shoe, we'd be on Boot Way, which is my block.

Would it be so wrong to run in for *two seconds* and warn my family about what's going on? I am not sure I should send them a Pegasus Post—it could be intercepted—and they need to know what I learned about Grandma Pearl and Alva. My family could be in danger. Who am I kidding? They *are* in danger. If Stiltskin wants to find me, he definitely will be after them. I need to get home. I walk faster and hope my friends will follow.

"Hey. This isn't the way to Pinocchio's Puppet Theatre," Maxine notices. "It's in the other direction."

"Is it?" Wilson looks up at me. I keep my eyes on the path ahead, sidestepping another bicycle lying in our way.

"Yeah, Gilly, this is the wrong way." Ollie points in the

opposite direction. "Pinocchio's Puppet Theatre is a few blocks away from Gnome-olia Bakery, and that's right off Baa, Baa, Black Sheep Boulevard. I mean, if we have time to get a few pattycakes on our way, that wouldn't hurt anyone."

"Except we really need to be on This Little Piggy Place," AG corrects him. "By Combing the Sea?" She sighs. "Maybe I could just pop in the shoppe for a second. I love their dragon-tooth combs."

"We are not going shopping or getting food! We need to get to school before those gargoyles come back and try to take us away," Jocelyn says. They all start arguing, which is the perfect time for me to break into a run. "Hey! Where are you going?"

"To see my family!" I yell, not looking back.

"You can't!" Jax yells. "It's not safe!"

"I'll be fine! You guys keep going. I'll meet up with you!" I promise.

"Gilly, watch out!" Ollie shouts, but it's too late.

I trip and go tumbling into a tent in someone's backyard. Wilson goes flying out of my pocket and lands in a piece of cake on the picnic blanket next to the tent. But I've landed hard and torn my red-and-white-striped tights, and my knee is bleeding. I get up slowly.

"Are you mad as a hatter?" Jocelyn barks. "You can't run off like that. We have to stick together."

"I'm sorry, but I've got the worst feeling about my family," I say, wiping off my knees. "I just wanted to check on them."

"You have a feeling? Are your ears tingling?" Kayla's eyes light up. "Maybe your fairy senses are kicking in!"

I touch my ear. No vibrations. "My ears aren't tingling. I'm just worried about them." I look at Jax. "I need to make sure they're okay." AG pours some water from the pitcher on the picnic blanket onto a napkin and hands it to me to dab at my bleeding knee. "Thanks."

"Headmistress Flora can send someone, but we can't go to the boot," Jax points out. "What if it's being watched?"

"Um, guys?" AG interrupts. "How is this man snoring through all this commotion?" She points to a large man lying on the lawn. His shirt is curled up, showing off his belly button. "Is he Rip Van Winkle or something?"

Ollie peels back the opening to the tent. Two kids are sleeping inside, clutching wooden horses. "You two okay?" Ollie asks and nudges their shoulders. They continue to snore. Peaches pushes aside their uneaten sandwiches and steals the apple they have, swallowing it whole.

Maxine looks back at us guiltily. "I have to work on her not stealing things. But who knows when she ate last?"

This time I feel a tingling at the back of my neck, but I don't think it's due to fairy powers. I think it's intuition.

"Wait a minute—" Kayla says at the same time I begin to piece together what is happening.

I spin around and look at the other lawns—two people are asleep on a porch, and a child is out cold on a swing. A dog in his doghouse is slumbering too. Wilson starts squeaking madly, and I know he's thinking the same thing I am. It's as if my heart constricts at the same time I hear a ringing in my ears.

"Stiltskin," I say aloud. I jump over the sleeping man and run as fast as I can through the other backyards to 2 Boot Way. I can hear my friends trying to stop me, but I need to reach my home before Rumpelstiltskin does. I round the corner to my block. It's eerily quiet, but there are no carriages parked out front, no cooking ladles (Stiltskin has flown on one before) or signs of magic anywhere. I run up the path with my friends at my heels and throw open the door.

CHAPTER 9

Choose a Side

My twin brothers, Han and Hamish, look up from where they're sitting on the floor playing with some knights. "Gilly!" They both rush to me.

"*Gilly!*" Trixie screams. She drops the flute she was playing in front of the fireplace and comes running as well. The three of them practically bowl me over with their hug. I squeeze back, but my eyes are peering around the living room, making sure no one is lurking in the shadows ready to attack.

Everything appears to be in order, and they aren't fast asleep. A fire is going, the smell of something delicious is wafting in from the kitchen, and Mother is getting up from her rocking chair, where I can see she was knitting a pair of bright-blue socks. Maybe nothing fishy is going on after all. Could half the village nap at the same time?

Father walks through the door between our home and his shop and sees us. "What are you doing here?" he asks at the same time Mother reaches me to join in on the hug.

"Let your sister breathe," she says to my siblings with a laugh. They back away, and she moves in for her own embrace. Mother looks deep into my eyes. "It's so good to see you, my darling girl. We didn't think you had visitor weekend again till next month." She spies the group of kids in the doorway and smiles. "Oh! And here you brought company!"

"Hello, Mrs. Cobbler." Jax extends his hand. "Jax Porter. It's nice to see you again."

"I remember you, Jax," Mother says. "And your friends too. Come in! Don't stand in the doorway."

"We can't stay," Maxine says apologetically and gives me a pointed look. Peaches waddles into the room and sits down on the rug by the fire, looking as if she feels the exact opposite. "We should have been back to school by now."

"I just need a few minutes," I beg my friends.

"*Quack!*" Peaches says, and I assume she's agreeing with me.

"Two," Jocelyn stresses as she shuts the door behind her and locks it. She opens the peephole. "I'll stay on guard."

"En garde! En garde!" Han and Hamish shout, brandishing pretend swords.

"Now, now," Mother scolds. "You know how I feel about weapons—even pretend ones." She winks at me. "We don't want to send any more children to Fairy Tale Reform School."

Father walks into the room again, carrying a tray with a pitcher of iced tea and glasses. He smirks. "Even if it was the best thing that ever happened to one of our daughters."

He pulls a wand out of his pocket and waves it over the drinks. The glasses freeze up, making the drinks icy cold. We all reach for a glass and guzzle it down. I was thirstier than I realized.

"Want me to make more?" he asks and takes his wand again.

"No!" Mother says and looks at me. "Your father has taken up wand studies again, and all he wants to do is whisk food and drinks into existence. It isn't right when we already have what we need in the boot."

Father frowns. "But how else can I practice?"

"You're taking classes again, Father?" I'm surprised. The

only work Father usually wants to focus on is shoe leathers and boot repairs.

"Yes." He places the silver wand on the table. "It's never too late to turn over a new leaf, right?" I nod. "I used to like learning how to use a wand from…my mother. I thought, why not try to learn again?"

"Good for you," I tell him, and Wilson squeaks in agreement.

No one notices Peaches swipe the wand until it's halfway down her throat.

"*Peaches!*" Maxine says in horror. "Give that back right now!"

"*Quack! Quack! Quack, quack, quack!*" Peaches says. I've never heard her talk back to Maxine before.

"What do you mean you're saving it for when Gilly really needs it?" Maxine asks. "It's not Gilly's!"

"It's okay, Maxine," Father tells her. "I've got others. I bought several."

"He can't do a spell to save his life and keeps blowing up his own wand," Mother whispers in my ear. I try hard not to laugh.

Peaches waddles away happily.

"Why do you all look so flushed?" Mother feels my head. "Are you getting ill? See? This is why I should always put on a bigger pot of stew. You never know when guests will drop in. You all need something to keep you strong and healthy!"

At the word *stew*, Wilson pokes his head out of my pocket again.

"Stew, glorious stew!" Han rubs his belly. "We eat a lot now that Father's selling shoes again."

"I was always selling shoes," Father says. "Just not as many as I do now."

"I got a new doll!" Trixie thrusts the floppy doll in my face and grins. I notice she's lost her two front teeth. "Isn't she pretty? Mother made her a new dress."

"She's very pretty," I say, my heartbeat slowly returning to normal. Nothing is out of order. But still, I feel a tingling at the back of my neck. Is that what Kayla meant by fairy intuition? It can't be. I'm just on edge. "So everything is okay? Nothing is the matter?"

"No." Mother looks at Father in alarm. "Should there be? The village has been on high alert since the warnings about *those people*." She hesitates to say what's going on in front of my smaller siblings. "But other than a few practice raids, we haven't seen or heard a thing."

"Who's at the door? Just hit the floor! Hide under the cupboard stairs, even if it's just Goldilocks and the three bears," Han and Hamish say in unison.

I look at Mother in confusion. "I find the rhyme drives the point home with them. They're young," she says. "Now what is going on?"

I glance at my siblings. "I am not sure I should say in front of you-know-who."

"Han? Hamish, is it?" AG pipes up. "I'm Allison Grace, and I've never been in a boot house before. We live in a pop-up castle."

Mother looks at me for understanding.

"Her parents are royalty—Beauty and Prince Sebastian, the former Beast." Mother nods knowingly.

"Could you show me your room? You too, Trixie." She offers her hand.

"We all share one, so that's easy!" Trixie takes AG's hand and leads her up the stairs. "It's a lot roomier now that Gilly and Anna aren't here."

Mother smiles sadly when she sees my reaction to hearing

Anna's name. "They're having a hard time with her being gone too," she says.

Father swallows hard. "We haven't found the right way to explain to them that their sister is…"

"A villain?" I blurt out. Mother and Father look shocked.

"Gilly." Maxine puts a hand on my arm. "You're upsetting them."

"They need to know the truth," I say, my voice hardening. "Anna is a villain. We can't deny it anymore. She had her chance to escape Stiltskin when we were in Cloud City, and instead she tricked me and sided with him. She's helping him cast a curse that will erase Enchantasia and all of us in it." Mother clutches her sewing needles to her heart. "That's why I'm here. To warn you. The Cobbler family is in danger. Grandma Pearl says—"

"Grandma Pearl?" Father interrupts. "How do you… Why do…" He looks at my mother. "How does she know who she is?"

Mother stands up straighter. "I gave Gilly her information. The children deserve to know their grandmother!" Father starts arguing with her.

"I went to see her," I say, and both of them look at me in

surprise. I touch the strand of pearls with the red vial around my neck. For some reason, the vial has started glowing. Maybe it knows it's no longer with its owner? "She's pretty cool."

"I'll say!" Ollie pipes up. Father gives him a look, and Ollie hangs his head. "Sorry."

"She told me about you as a child, Father, and how we can use our fairy ancestry to hone our gifts to form a quorum and stop this curse."

Father puts his hand up. "Enough. I have never felt like a fairy. And I don't want to talk about my mother."

"Why do so many fairy tales have mother issues?" Maxine whispers.

"Father, please. You have to listen." I try again. "Alva and Grandma Pearl were best friends till Grandma betrayed her. Alva cursed her not to love. That's why she abandoned you. She's had a protection charm over her this whole time, but now she's given it to me. My teachers say Rumpelstiltskin's villain book shows our family is wrapped up in this curse somehow, and we can stop it. If we just try to focus on our fairy traits—"

"No," he says.

"You should come with us to Fairy Tale Reform School to help stop him," I continue to try.

"I'm not leaving my shoppe!" Father argues.

"You'll be safer at the school," I say. "Stiltskin is looking for me, and if he's looking for me, he's got to be looking for all of you too." Father is suddenly quiet.

"We have to keep the children safe," Mother says. "If Gilly's right…"

"I don't trust anything my mother says," Father disagrees. "She left me when I was smaller than the twins. She doesn't even know us."

"That doesn't mean she doesn't love us in her own way," Mother says.

"If Alva is after us, let her come," Father insists. "She already has one of my daughters at her side. How much worse can it get?"

"Much worse," Jocelyn speaks up. "Considering she wants to erase all of us."

"Yeah, but didn't Anna say Stiltskin agreed to keep the Cobbler family around?" Ollie asks.

"And you believe he will?" Jax is incredulous.

Everyone is talking over one another. I try to get a word

in, but no one is listening. Suddenly I hear a bloodcurdling scream.

"Trixie!" I bound up the stairs, the others at my heels. I reach the top step and BAM! I get thrown backward. I look up in surprise.

A crackling, bright-yellow force field separates me from the landing to my siblings' bedroom. The shimmering wall of magic is transparent so I can see exactly who is on the other side.

The Stiltskin Squad.

Led by my sister Anna.

AG, Trixie, Han, and Hamish are trapped on the other side of the force field with them. I wait for AG to transform into the she-wolf I know she can be in times of trouble, but she doesn't. Then I realize why: she's been immobilized midscream. The Squad grabs the boys and Trixie and starts pushing them toward the window. Trixie is in tears, but the twins are too confused to understand what is going on.

"Get away from them!" I shout as Jocelyn shoots a fireball at the wall. It ricochets and nearly takes my father's head off.

"Get down!" Jax shouts to my parents. He fumbles for his pocket watch.

"Don't," I whisper, pushing him behind me so the squad doesn't see him trying to retaliate. "We may still need that."

"The children! Gilly! Do something!" Mother cries.

My heart is beating fast. My beloved younger sister, Anna, is walking toward the force field that separates us. Her brown hair is longer and wavier than it was a few months ago, and her FTRS uniform has long been abandoned for a tan jumpsuit, belted at her thin waist. We stare at each other.

"*Quack!*" Peaches waddles up the stairs and starts to dry heave. Next thing I know, Father's wand, miniaturized, is lying at my feet, covered in saliva. I pick up the wand and wipe it off on my skirt. Will it still work in this size?

Hansel bursts out laughing. "What are you going to do with that thing? Make a mouse house?"

Wilson pokes his head out and starts squeaking madly.

I concentrate hard on bringing the wall between us down, aiming the wand at the force field. "Retract!" I shout. A small hole begins to burn in the center of the shield. The squad starts to look nervous. If I keep going, it's going to come down. "Retract!" I yell again, aiming at the same spot, but this time the beam shoots straight through and comes dangerously close to hitting my brothers. The pair of them scream.

"What are you doing?" Anna says. "You're scaring them!"

"*You're* scaring them!" I counter. "Let them go."

"I knew you'd come," Anna says with a sneer. "You just can't stay away from home."

"Unlike you," I spit out. Maxine coughs. She hates when I'm mean—even to my double-crossing sibling. "You should go or things will get ugly." My hand is on the mirror in my pocket to call for backup. "You may be a villain now, but even a villain wouldn't harm their family."

Anna flinches as if the word hurts her as much as it hurts me. "I would never hurt… You don't understand!"

I throw my hands up. "What don't I understand, Anna? How you felt left behind when I was *sentenced* to Fairy Tale Reform School? How you felt left out when Mother and Father were proud that I *reformed*? That you felt I had abandoned you because I wanted to better *myself* at school? Get over yourself!" I snap, finally having had enough. "Not everything is about you!" She winces. "I'm trying to help save Enchantasia while you try to destroy it."

"You don't—"

"Understand," I interrupt. "Yes, you keep saying that."

I pull an arrow out of my pack and nock it. "Now go or I'll take this whole force field down with my...magic arrows."

"You have magic arrows?" Maxine whispers. Jocelyn stomps on her foot.

Anna raises an eyebrow. "I'd like to see you try. I'm not leaving till I get what I came for. I'm just surprised you didn't figure out what I was up to earlier. Half the village is asleep."

"That was you!" Kayla says. "I knew it!"

Anna stands up straighter. "I know lots of spells now. No thanks to any of you. The only reason I didn't put a sleeping spell on this house is because I needed everyone awake." Her eyes flicker to our mother.

Mother steps forward. "Anna Bear, stop this at once. This isn't you. Come home."

"Let us help you," Father adds, his voice soft. Trixie, Han, and Hamish are still crying.

"Mama? Why's she doing this?" I hear Han's small voice, and it nearly breaks my heart.

Anna looks away. "It's too late to help me. I need to finish this and get what I came for."

Hansel and Gretel move toward the force field, coming straight toward me. "Drop the barrier, Heidi," Hansel tells the girl who is concentrating on the magic that keeps us apart. "I'm tired of listening to this. Let's just take her now."

I hold the wand at the ready. "You're not taking anyone." I step closer to the force field. I can hear it sizzling. "Leave now before you regret coming here."

Hansel and Gretel do the opposite, a look of hatred written all over their faces.

I keep my eyes trained on Anna and the squad. "Jax? Maxine? Get my parents to safety. Jocelyn? When the barrier comes down, get AG. Ollie, help me with my siblings. I can take care of myself."

Anna laughs. "Of course, you can. It was me who couldn't, and you left me out here alone." Her face hardens. "I would never do that to you or my family. What I'm doing is for all of us."

"*You're helping a villain!*" I shout.

"Girls, that is enough," Father interrupts, but Anna is looking at me curiously.

"Drop the barrier like she wants. I'm not scared of fighting her," Anna says.

Heidi looks briefly at Anna. "But Stiltskin said—"

"I know what he said," Anna snaps. "Drop the barrier."

The girl lowers her hands, and the barrier begins to fade away. I hold the wand ready to zap Anna or anyone else who tries to hurt my siblings.

Anna holds up her wand, and the two of us face each other. As soon as the barrier drops, we both send sparks flying at the same time. They hit one another and bounce back, causing a huge hole in the bedroom wall. Jocelyn hurls three fireballs in quick succession that knock several squad members to the floor. Hansel and Gretel get their wands blown out of their hands by Kayla's quick wand work.

"Retreat! Retreat! They're gaining on us!" I hear Hansel shout. "We will come back for her!"

"No!" Anna cries stubbornly, her eyes ablaze in the flames. She and I aim at each other again. I fire first and hit her in the shoulder. I see her stumble backward in surprise. In the middle of the firing, I spot a clear path to my brothers and Trixie. I take it, dashing toward them. Han sees me and holds his arms out wide to grab me.

But before I can reach him, Hansel fires, and the blast hits me in the thigh. I falter for mere seconds and watch in horror as Hansel yanks both boys toward him. He knocks them down and throws a magic bean on the bedroom floor.

I watch in horror as a portal opens in the floor, a swirling vortex of yellow light funneling into the unknown.

"What are you doing?" Anna cries.

"Making her come to us!" With a sick smile, Hansel pushes Han and Hamish in before I can even scream. Gretel, Heidi, and some of the others jump in after him.

"*No!*" I cry as Anna leaps for the portal before I can reach it.

She dives in as it closes up. Father and Mother reach the spot at the same time I do, but the portal is already gone. I slide across the floor feeling for an opening, but I know already there's none. My brothers are gone.

"Mama!" Trixie cries, diving into my mother's arms.

"Where'd they go?" Father thunders, stomping the floor as though looking for a trapdoor. The others rush forward as AG collapses like jelly onto the floor. Ollie and Maxine help her up. "Where are they?" Father screams.

"Gone," I whisper.

I've lost my brothers to Anna. How could I have been so foolish as to come here? She knew I'd come home for them. They were the perfect bait, and I fell for it.

"Gilly, watch out!" Kayla cries as a gargoyle comes crashing through a window, a Stiltskin Squad member on its back. Another gargoyle comes roaring through the opposite window, and a Stiltskin Squad member jumps off and comes running toward us, shooting her wand. Father grabs Mother and Trixie, and Jax ushers them down the steps as the wand fire keeps coming. Jocelyn gets off a few more fireballs and one hits the ceiling, setting it ablaze. Maxine and Ollie drag me to my feet before my childhood bed goes up in flames. Three more gargoyles and squad members come flying through the broken windows.

A boy with dark eyes sees me and grins. "Get her."

CHAPTER 10

Fight or Flight

ᔐᔑ

The squad members and gargoyles cross the flames in the bedroom and come racing toward us. Jocelyn shoots fireballs in their direction to hold them off. A gargoyle swoops across the room, coming dangerously close to grabbing my father as he's the last one down the boot stairs. Kayla stuns the creature with a wave of her wand and hurries down after them as the roof catches fire. Wilson is squeaking madly in my ear, but he sounds far away.

I know I should move, but I can't. Anna kidnapped my brothers. She is helping Rumpelstiltskin destroy Enchantasia. It finally occurs to me that there might be nothing I can do to stop this.

And I've never been more frightened.

Jax slides onto the floor next to me as arrows and flame balls fly past our heads. "Thief?" He stares into my eyes. "We've got to go."

The first time I saw Jax, he was swinging from a chandelier while trying to break out of Fairy Tale Reform School. I'd never met someone with violet eyes before. Or fancied myself someone who could be friends with a prince. But right now, I don't want to listen to him.

I curl into a ball, still not moving. "Anna has Han and Hamish."

"Yes. And sitting on this burning floor isn't going to bring them back." Jax offers me his hand. "We'll find them, but first we have to get out of here. Kayla has your family, Ollie grabbed AG, and Maxine and Jocelyn are holding off the squad. The only person left to take care of is you."

I feel like I'm going to cry. "But I didn't take care of them."

"You will," Jax says as I hear Jocelyn screaming for me in the background. Jax stays calm. "We will get them back. Trust me."

I want to. Badly. But as the smoke overtakes the room, it feels so easy to give up. I had my chance to grab Anna, and instead, once again, I let her get away. Grandma Pearl is right—she can't be saved.

You can still save Han and Hamish! You can stop this curse! But you have to get off that floor!

Who said that? I wonder. It doesn't matter. The voice shakes me from this trance. I reach for Jax's hand.

Then I see a gargoyle swooping toward us. I yank my hand back, knocking Jax sideways just as the beastie's claws try to sink into his shoulders. I forgot how bad those things stink.

"I saved you," I tell Jax. "Now we're even."

He shakes his head and helps me up.

"The boot is coming down!" a squad member shouts to the others still battling Jocelyn and Maxine. "Let's get out of here!" The squad member grabs hold of a gargoyle and gets pulled out the window to safety.

"Wait!" Another squad member points to me. "He said not to leave without her!"

A gargoyle swoops toward me, and I grab an arrow from the quiver on the floor. I quickly nock it, ready to fire, but a burning beam from the ceiling falls in front of me, blocking the rest of the squad from view. The smoke is becoming so thick, I can hardly see.

"Come on!" Jax shouts and pulls me toward what's left of the window. Maxine grabs Peaches, and she and Jocelyn disappear over the ledge. My heart is pounding as I look around. My family home is in flames. Jax pulls my hand, and I leap away from the flames licking at my boots.

Seconds later, I land on a flying carpet that takes us away from the fire.

"Perfect timing, Blue!" Jax says. The blue, green, and gold rug has come to our aid before. Blue zooms over the Dwarf Police Squad where I see dwarves streaming out of the building and people rushing out of their homes. Whatever spell Anna placed on them has lifted. Blue touches down near the fountain in the crowded village square. Some people are hugging, others are crying. I jump off Blue, and Mother and Father grab me as Trixie cries into my skirt. Several people run by talking about Stiltskin. The village is in a panic.

"The boys," I start to say but Mother shushes me.

"One thing at a time." She holds me tight, but I don't feel any better.

I see AG with a blanket wrapped around her, and I let go of Mother to sit by AG at the fountain.

"Are you okay?" I ask.

"Yes, but Anna. Your brothers. I'm sorry." AG starts to cough, and Kayla holds her up.

"Just rest," I tell her. I look at Kayla and Maxine worriedly.

"Whatever spell they cast really affected her," Kayla whispers to me. "She should be looked at right away."

A crack of thunder booms in the distance. Clouds are rolling in thick and fast. I hear the sound of bells and know Pete and the Dwarf Police Squad must finally be checking on my family's burning boot. They're always a few paces behind.

"We need to get AG back to her parents at the castle," Ollie says. "Can we borrow Blue? How'd he even get here?"

"I thought you sent for him," Jax says to Ollie.

Ollie frowns. "No, I thought you did."

Blue snuggles up next to me, one of his gold tassels stroking my chin. "Maybe he just knows when we need him."

"He's a rug," Jocelyn retorts. "He doesn't have feelings." Blue's tassel smacks her on the arm. "Ouch!"

I feel for my mirror and find my sheath empty. "The mirror is gone! I must have lost it in the boot."

"Great. Now we have no way to reach the school and let them know what happened," Jocelyn says, slumping down on the fountain and rubbing her arm where she now has rug burn.

"Yes we do," Jax says as he helps Ollie carry AG over to Blue and gently places her on the carpet. "Blue will take AG back to school with Ollie. He'll tell the professors everything when he takes AG back right now. She can't go alone in her condition."

"I'll go too," Kayla says and looks at me. "I should see what else Mother has learned about the Fire Moon. If we really are going to need a quorum, maybe I can rally more fairies to help us."

"That's a good idea," I tell her.

She takes my hands in her own. "Concentrate on your fairy abilities. I know you have it in you!" she insists. "They will keep you strong and guide you till you're back to school." She hugs me. "Be safe."

"You too," I tell her.

There's more thunder in the distance. "You better get going before the storm," Jocelyn suggests, and we watch as Blue carries Ollie, Kayla, and AG into the air.

"*Quack!*" Peaches nestles in Maxine's arms.

Maxine's eyes are on the sky. "Peaches is right. What if the gargoyles come back?"

"Let's keep moving," I suggest. "We need to get to Pinocchio's and find that secret passageway back to school." I look at my parents and sister. "You're coming with us." They start to protest. "It's not safe for you to stay in the village."

"Besides, where will you go?" Jocelyn asks my mother. "Your boot is one big piece of burnt shoe leather right now."

Trixie bursts into tears again. I give Jocelyn a look and kneel down by my sister. "Trix, I know this is hard, but we need to be brave. What did Anna say to you before we got upstairs?"

She scrunches up her tiny face, which is covered in freckles. "She kept saying, 'I won't hurt you. It's going to be okay.' They wanted to take all of us, but she said they only needed you. And then Hansel said if they couldn't catch you, they'd take us anyway as it would make you come find us. They said they'd win either way."

Jocelyn scratches her chin. "It's an impressive villain

move, actually. If they need you for the curse, you're going to come right to them now that they have your brothers."

"I keep messing up!" I cry and look at my father. "If I had gotten to you sooner, the boys would be safe and the boot wouldn't be gone." Then I remember Father's workshop attached to the boot. "Your business… It was going so well."

Mother dabs her eye with a handkerchief. "Your father did manage to grab these on our way out." Mother opens the sack on her arm and pulls out a red velvet box. She opens the lid. A pair of shiny glass slippers are inside. "The royal court's latest order. We aren't sure who they were meant for, but at least there is one pair left."

Those shoes are the whole reason I wound up in FTRS to begin with. Royal Academy's beloved Fairy Godmother started conjuring pairs up on her own and caused Father to almost go out of business. I started stealing to help buy food for my family, wound up in FTRS, and the rest is history. Now my family is back at square one.

"There is no need to despair!" Father says, interrupting my thoughts. "We will rebuild." Father puts his arm around Mother. "We'll make a bigger boot, with a larger workshop.

It really doesn't matter where we're cobblers as long as we're together." He places his hands on my shoulders. "I know I've been hard on you in the past, but this isn't your fault. You need to stop blaming yourself for everything. A problem this big can't rest entirely on one person's shoulders."

I nod. Father is right, but it's easier said than done. I know I need to listen to my friends more and follow my gut. But what if both of those things are still not enough? The thunder booms louder.

"We need to get to Pinocchio's before it rains." Jax eyes the darkening sky.

We make our way through the crowded streets. Someone is already selling the latest edition of *Happily Ever After Scrolls* and offering instant scroll downloads on the "attack on the Cobbler family." We hurry past, staying close together and keeping our eyes on the clouds for signs of gargoyles.

"There's our boot," Trixie points to a painting of our home up in flames that is flashing on a mini magical scroll. Scrolls all around the village square light up with pictures of our boot's charred remains: COBBLER HOME IN RUINS. IS RUMPELSTILTSKIN TO BLAME?

"Is it true?" A woman grabs Mother's arm. "Is Rumpelstiltskin here? Is that why we were all fast asleep?"

"I thought Old Man Rip Van Winkle would try a move like that, not him," says another man. "Where is Rumpelstiltskin now?"

"We haven't seen him," I say and usher my parents away. We can't get caught up in conversations. Getting back to school with my remaining family is all the more important now. We keep walking, but everyone is staring at us.

"Faster! Faster!" Maxine whispers.

"Now's when I really wish you knew how to fly," Jocelyn grumbles to me.

I look at Father. "Have you ever… Did you learn how to…fly?" I ask awkwardly.

Now is probably not the time to ask, but what if we're out of time?

Father looks at me briefly, then looks straight ahead. "Your grandmother tried to teach me, but I didn't want to learn. Besides, not every fairy learns that skill—especially if they don't believe in it."

"I believe, I believe," I hear Trixie whisper. She looks up

at me and smiles. "If I could fly, I'd be able to see over the treetops! I'd find Han and Hamish."

"We will find them," I promise, whisking her along. I'm so anxious about getting back to school that my heart is beating out of my chest. A long, low rumble of thunder makes everyone jump. The sky looks like it will open any minute. Finally, I see Pinocchio's Puppet Theatre up ahead. Maxine hurries to the front door and tries the knob.

She starts to drool. "It's closed!"

Jax pounds on the door, then looks in the windows. "No one is in there."

I try one of the windows, but it's locked. "I guess they got spooked by the sleeping curse and closed early. Now what? Do we break in?"

"We do not break into someone's shoppe," Mother says sternly. "There must be another way to get to school quickly."

Jocelyn and I look at each other. "Pegasi."

We hurry down the street again, going straight to the Pegasus stables, but I stop short when I see the huge line. People are carrying babies, holding chickens or goats on leashes, and carrying huge boxes. Children are crying, and the place is pandemonium. All the Pegasus stalls are empty.

One of the workers comes running over. "Don't get in line!" Sweat beads on his forehead. A gold badge on his shirt tells me his name is Chaz, and he has a three-year award for good flying service. "I keep telling these people, the last ride already left! Everyone is trying to flee the village." He looks at my parents. "You're the Cobblers! What happened at your boot? Is Rumpelstiltskin here? Did he cast the curse?" He grabs Father's jacket.

"Calm down, young man! Rumpelstiltskin is not here!" Father barks, and the worker lets go of him. "When are the Pegasi due back?"

The worker's eyes widen. "They're not. Everyone wants to leave Enchantasia Village now, the Pegasi included."

"Don't be silly," Maxine says. "Pegasi don't flee...do they?"

"You're leaving, aren't yuh?" he asks.

Maxine looks at the rest of us. "Yes, but um, we have somewhere important we need to be." She gulps hard. "Where are they going?" She looks at the long lines. "It's not like there is anywhere safe...is there?"

"My sister in Sherwood Forest says there's no gargoyles there," says a troll in line with triplets running circles around him. "We are camping out there."

"I heard Avalon is a safer bet," says a man carrying two suitcases and a parrot cage. "No one messes with that king."

"Wonderland is where I'm going," says a kid in a Jack of All Trades School uniform. "That queen may cut off people's heads, but she's not trying to rewrite history." He taps the Pegasus stable worker on the shoulder. "When are more Pegasi coming back? When?"

"I told you, kid, just like I told the others," Chaz says. "Go home! There's no way out of Enchantasia by air unless you've got a magic carpet."

"They're sold out already!" says a blond girl in a Royal Academy sash carrying multiple shopping bags. "I knew I shouldn't have left the castle! Who's going to rescue me now?"

I roll my eyes. Classic blondie. "You can rescue yourself," I say. "Find another way back. That's what we're going to do." I look at the others. "What's our plan? Walk?"

"That will take forever," Maxine groans.

"Do you have a better idea?" Jocelyn snaps.

"You don't have to be mean about it," Maxine complains and the two start arguing. Peaches gets in between them and starts quacking madly. "What about the storm?" I hear Maxine say, but the storm is already here.

A loud crack of thunder followed by a lightning bolt flashing across the sky make everyone look up. Trixie starts to cry, as do the other kids in line. I wait for fat raindrops to fall, but none come, even though the sky is as dark as I've ever seen it. Suddenly, I see the trees near the stables begin to bow in the wind. Within seconds, dead leaves are blowing across the street, along with parchments and someone's lunch bag. I'm about to say, "We should look for cover," when a giant gust of wind whooshes through the street so fiercely that people fall over.

We grab hold of one another, trying to stay upright, and I hear what sounds like cannon fire from a ship. The boom is so loud, my ears ring. I look around, wondering where it's coming from, when I see something strange. The air is waffling in front of my eyes, much as it did in my boot, but this time shock waves wash over the village. It comes straight toward us, and I feel the cold sensation wash over me. A second later, the skies clear and the storm is gone. I look around at the others in wonder.

"Uh, Gilly?" Trixie is pulling on my uniform. "Why do they all look so mad?"

I look back at everyone in line. They're glaring at us.

Chaz's face is equally angry. "There are the villains he's after! Get them!"

CHAPTER 11

Friend or Foe?

U s? Villains?" Maxine points to herself as Peaches quacks madly. "You've got this all wrong!"

A woman in line holding a baby screams. "Help! Someone! Call the police chief!"

"Wait, we're not villains," Trixie tries to explain as an angry mob of villagers led by Chaz heads toward us. Father pushes Trixie and Mother behind him. "Rumpelstiltskin is!"

"How dare you? He's a good man!" the woman holding the baby shouts.

Jax and I back into each other as the mob starts to surround us. "Stiltskin must have made his second wish," he says. "Now he's good and we're the hunted."

"Darlene would never agree to that wish!" Maxine insists

as we cling to one another with nowhere left to go. "She couldn't."

"She has no choice," Jocelyn reminds Maxine. "He must have realized there are wish loopholes...or figured out some of them."

Maxine hangs her head. "Poor Darlene."

"Poor Darlene? Poor us!" I say as the mob inches in closer. I look for a way to escape, but there is none. Blue is on his way back to FTRS, if he hasn't been accosted. The Pegasi are all gone, and we'll never get away on foot in such a big group.

I hear galloping and see Pete and his guards come roaring up on horses, their crossbows drawn. Pete's eyes narrow when he sees me. "You have nerve showing up here, villains. You won't cast your curse here! You are hereby sentenced to life in the dungeons by order of the royal court. Drop your weapons." Pete looks at Jocelyn. "You lift your hand to fire, and you will take a crossbow to the heart. You hear me?"

I wince. Pete is annoying but never cruel.

"And you three!" He points to Jax, Maxine, and me. "Hand over those bows and arrows, that pocket watch and the sword." I hesitate, wondering if I should hold on to the mini wand. I take a chance and just give Pete my bow and arrows.

"What's happening?" Trixie asks. "Why do they think we're the bad guys?"

We throw our weapons in a pile, and Pete dismounts along with the rest of his officers to retrieve them. Then they draw their crossbows on us again. I'm not sure how we're going to get out of this one.

BOOM!

An explosion rocks the Pegasi stable, setting it ablaze and sending the mob running for cover. *BOOM! BOOM!* More explosions land around the stable, destroying the Pegasi corral and the waiting line. I hear a whizzing sound as another hit lands. Smoke blankets the area, making it impossible to see and causing everyone to start coughing.

"I can't see!" Pete shouts. "Don't let them get away!"

I feel a hand on my arm. It's a girl's.

"Come with me! Quickly now!" she whispers. She's wearing a blue cloak, and her hood casts a shadow on her face. Jax and Jocelyn look at me. Red? There's no time to be sure, but we don't really have any other options. The smoke is already starting to disperse. "Come! Follow me!"

"Where are they?" I hear a dwarf guard shout.

"Spread out!"

I link hands with Trixie and my mother, while Father holds on to Maxine. I can see Jax and Jocelyn up ahead, right behind the woman in blue. She rounds the next street and pushes us behind her as more guards go running by.

"We have to find them!"

"The fire brigade is coming for the blaze!"

Once they're gone, the girl moves again, turning left, then right before squeezing down a narrow alleyway. Empty boxes marked BAKING YEAST, FLOUR, and SPRINKLES litter the walkway. We must be behind Gnome-olia Bakery. The girl has her back toward us as she feels along the brick wall. Every once in a while, she turns her attention to the alleyway. I hear a siren in the distance and more shouting.

"Gilly," Mother whispers in my ear. "I taught you not to talk to strangers. Should we be following this girl down an alleyway?"

Mother has a point.

I clear my throat. "Thanks for getting us out of that—"

"Shh!" she says. "They'll hear you!"

The girl presses a finger to a brick above a sign that says GNOME MORE FREE HANDOUTS. IF YOU WANT IT, BUY IT! and I hear a click. The bricks in front of us slowly recede into the darkness, and an opening forms. The girl walks inside and disappears down the staircase.

"Come on!" she whispers. "Quickly! The door only stays open so long."

Mother keeps Trixie behind her and doesn't move. Jocelyn forms a fireball in her hand, but doesn't launch it. The back of my neck is tingling, and I can't tell if that's a good sign or a bad one.

"Where does this lead?" I ask, and she doesn't say anything. "Answer us. How do we know this isn't a trap too?"

"Yeah, how do we know you're not on his side?" Jocelyn asks, and there is a chorus of "yeahs."

The girl emerges from the shadows and lowers her hood, revealing her long, blond hair. "Because I'm on yours."

I gasp. Princess Rose?

She is *not* on our side. She's the sleeping beauty who tried to take over Enchantasia long before Rumpelstiltskin came back to town! She once poisoned me with gingerroot and held me hostage, and she brainwashed the Royal Ladies-in-Waiting! I grab the nearest weapon I can find—a broken rolling pin in the alley—and brandish it at her. "You come one step closer, and I'll…throw this at your head!"

"Gilly! You mind your manners," Mother says. "Princess Rose is royalty."

"Royalty who tried to turn in the Royal Academy students that Fairy Godmother Olivina outlawed," Jax points out as he blocks my family from harm. "Rapunzel told me what you tried to do."

Jocelyn holds her fireball ready. "Anyone who sides with villains is a villain." She pauses before firing. "Hey. Why weren't you affected by Stiltskin's wish?"

Rose awkwardly plays with her hair. "Maybe because my mind tends to go to the dark side sometimes, which means I act villainous already."

"See?" I motion to the others. I hear more blasts and shouting in the distance. The dwarves are going to find us at any moment.

"But I'm not a villain." Rose's eyes water. "At least I don't want to be. When Stiltskin showed up at the royal court compound and took over, I could see what a menace he truly was."

"So he's there now?" Jax asks.

Rose nods. "Yes. It's where he pushed that nice genie to grant his first wish—to track you. And then when he didn't catch you, he made his second one—a wish to make the people of the kingdom think you're the enemies. Darlene explained it wouldn't work on people who were already a little wicked, so I suspect everyone at FTRS, like yourselves, would be immune, plus your family, who truly loves you and would never see you as the enemy. But the rest of the kingdom is on the hunt for you." Rose's eyes begin to water. "Stiltskin knew the Royal Court would try to stop them, so he banished the rest of the princesses to another land by magic bean. I'm the only one still here." She looks at me. "And we can't let him get his hands on you. For some reason, he and Alva want to find you before the Fire Moon."

I can't believe I'm thinking this, but my gut tells me Rose is telling the truth.

Rose looks at Jax. "Your sister got word to Headmistress Flora to let him know what was happening, but she couldn't get everyone out of harm's way before the wish. She knew someone needed to find you all and get you to safety. I was their only hope. That was the last thing she said to me before…"

"I don't buy it," Jocelyn says. "Where does this tunnel lead to anyway?"

"Your school. The former Wicked Stepmother doesn't

know *every* secret in this kingdom," Rose says coolly and looks at me. "You don't think Ella would let Flora create a villain school and not have more than one secret way into it in case of emergency?"

"Makes sense," I admit.

"These tunnels are large and tricky, but as long as you stay on the yellow path, you'll make it back to school. I've used this path before when... Well, it doesn't matter. You can take this straight back to school, and no one will be able to find you. Now go!" Her blue eyes light up defiantly. "I'll stay back to close up the passage and hold them off."

"They went this way!" I hear someone shout and know the guards are getting closer.

"You don't believe her, do you?" Jocelyn asks me.

"I don't know." Rose has double-crossed people many times before, but now we're out of options.

"Everyone deserves redemption," my mother says quietly. She looks at me. "Isn't that what your school is all about?"

Rose's pink lips curve into a deep frown as she looks at me. "Look, I know trying to help you now doesn't make up for what I've done in the past, but I *do* want to help you.

I don't know why he needs you for this curse, but we can't allow him to erase Enchantasia's past. If anyone can stop him, Gillian, I believe it's you."

There's more shouting in the streets, and the *click-clack* of horseshoes on the pavement grows louder.

"Okay," I say, and Rose breathes a sigh of relief. I push Father's last pair of glass slippers toward her. "But if you're lying, I will not rest till I find you and...and...ruin every last pair of shoes you own."

"Gillian," Father says harshly. In our boot, destroying shoes is no joking matter.

Rose winces and clutches the box. "Deal."

Maxine and Peaches head into the passageway, leading my parents and sister along with them. Kayla ducks in after them and Jocelyn follows, disappearing down the stairs.

"There they are!" Pete shouts. I see the men pushing and shoving to get through the alleyway.

Rose pulls up her hood, holds out her wand, and stands tall. "Go. Now."

Jax and I climb into the opening and look back at Rose curiously.

Maybe people can change if they want to bad enough. I guess I'm proof of that.

"Princess Rose?" I call. "Thank you."

I think I see her smile as she pushes on a brick and the opening closes up behind us, enveloping us in darkness.

CHAPTER 12

Tunnel Vision

A nd we're *sure* this is the way to school?" Maxine asks as we continue along the damp, narrow tunnel. Peaches is walking slightly ahead of us. "Because it feels like we've been walking in circles *forever*."

"Think about how long it takes to get from the village to school by Pegasi," Jax says as he leads the way, breaking through another cobweb in our path. "It could take hours for us to arrive at FTRS."

"If we're even headed to FTRS," Jocelyn complains again. "We have no clue if Rose was telling the truth about the yellow path." She turns around and glares at me, her face bright red in the glow of her fireball. "I can't believe you trusted her."

"She's been a very good customer," Father pipes up as he readjusts Trixie, who is riding along on his back.

"She didn't have to show up in the village when she did and get us out of that jam," I remind Jocelyn. "Sometimes you have to take a leap of faith."

"Your leaps of faith have cost us in the past," Jocelyn grumbles.

I'm slightly satisfied when several drops of water drip onto her face at that exact moment. The tunnel is full of condensation and it smells like fish, but we are completely alone and safe. *I think.*

"We have no idea what's happening above us, what time it is, or whether Stiltskin has made any more wishes," Jocelyn adds. "What if he wishes to find the harp pieces? Huh?"

The rest of us are silent. The only sound is the drip, drip, dripping of water and bats or rats squeaking in the (I hope) distance.

Jocelyn has a point. What *if* Stiltskin wishes to find the harp pieces? He's already got the lamp. He's made us enemies of the kingdom. Why hasn't he wished himself the remaining ingredients for his curse? That's what I'd do if I were in his shoes. Something about her question is haunting me. I just can't put my finger on what it is.

"Even if he does, he'd still have to wait for the Fire Moon," Maxine reminds us. "He can't do anything till then. We still have time to stop him." She looks around. "As long as we can find our way out of these tunnels."

Wilson begins to squeak madly. I think I understand what he's saying.

"You want to be put down and look for a way out?" I ask. He squeaks some more. "But what if I can't find you?" Wilson continues to squeak. "You'll find me? Okay. Be careful and stick to the yellow path," I say and place him on the tunnel floor. He takes off into the darkness.

"Look at that!" Jocelyn points to the floor. "The yellow line is so faded I can't tell if we're supposed to go left or right from here. This is pointless! We're stuck here. And how are we going to face our end? In a stinky tunnel."

Father and Jax shed light on the yellow line using my mini wand. It's true: You can't tell if we're meant to go left or right at this point. If we go the wrong way, we could wind up anywhere or be lost down here forever.

"I have no clue which way we go," Father says and slumps down against the wall.

"Let's take a break for a minute. I'm exhausted," Mother says and sits down next to him. Jocelyn and Jax do the same, but Trixie is still staring at the paths.

I put an arm on her small shoulder. "What are you thinking?"

She keeps looking at the floor. "I think we go left. I'm not sure why, but I can feel it, like here, in the back of my neck. It's like a little voice telling me, 'Left, left, left!'" She smiles at me, revealing the gap in her front teeth.

In the back of my neck. Is Trixie embracing her fairy traits? I stare at the two paths, just like her, and wait for something to come to me. At first I feel nothing. My mind is full of thoughts of curses and Stiltskin and the end of the kingdom as we know it. *Concentrate*, I hear Grandma Pearl saying. *Focus.* So this time I close my eyes, not even looking at the path. I listen to the sound of my breathing, and I think of Fairy Tale Reform School. Suddenly, the tunnels' paths appear in my mind. The left one starts to glow.

"It is left!" I say, opening my eyes in surprise. "I saw it!"

Trixie nods. "Glowing? Me too! In my head!"

Mother smiles at Father. "Looks like your children are embracing their fairy heritage."

Father gives me a curious glance. "Mm-hmm."

"Everyone up!" I say excitedly. "Follow us!"

We head down the path, Peaches waddling beside me. It feels like we are walking forever before I see a small light at the end of the tunnel. "Look!" I run ahead and point out the round steel door at the end of the path. In the center of the door is a wheel that is rusted over and has seen better days. "Hmm. It doesn't look like this door has been used in ages."

Jax gives it a twist. "It's...pretty...tight... I...can't... turn...it."

"Put some muscle into it, Prince!" Jocelyn tells him, and I give her a look.

"Let me help you," Father says, putting Trixie down.

The two of them yank and get nowhere. Jocelyn fires up a fireball.

"Don't!" I cry. "It will rebound."

"Well, what do we do now?" Jocelyn says in exasperation. "We have no way of reaching anyone down here! We'll have to turn back."

"Nooooo," Trixie moans. "I can't walk anymore."

"And you didn't even walk the whole way," Mother points out.

"We could try banging on the door," I suggest. "If the door is inside FTRS, maybe someone on the other side will hear us."

We walk over to the door and brush aside more of the cobwebs, scaring the spiders away from their webs. Then we all start pounding.

"Help!" Maxine shouts, her hand so heavy the door actually vibrates when she makes contact. "We're locked out!"

We stop knocking and listen. Silence.

Jax sinks down on the wall. "Well, we might as well wait here and take a nap or work and try knocking again in a little while." He pulls a piece of parchment out of his jacket. "Does anyone have a quill?"

"Do not tell me you're doing homework right now," I say.

"I do!" Trixie pulls one out of her pocket and hands it to him.

"Why not?" Jax puts the quill to paper. "It's not like we have anything better to do." He scribbles furiously. "How do you spell 'exemplary'?"

Mother spells it for him, then looks at me. "Did you do your assignment yet?"

"Not exactly," I say, and she and Father look at me. "But the assignment from Professor Sebastian isn't due till the end of the term."

"But term ends soon," Father reminds me. "And you haven't started yet?"

"If you haven't noticed, I've been kind of busy—trying to save Enchantasia and all."

"That doesn't mean you neglect your studies," Father says. "If the professor feels you have time to do a paper, then you should have time to do a paper."

"Dad," I huff. "You don't understand!"

Jocelyn pops up between us. "I already handed mine in, Mr. Cobbler. So did Maxine. I bet Ollie is back at school right now working on his too. You should really start yours, Gilly." She smiles sweetly.

Now she's just trying to get me in trouble. "Maybe we should focus on getting out of here and worry about our papers later." I start banging again. "Help! Can anyone hear us? We're stuck down here! Help!"

But no one comes.

We wait so long that I finally fall asleep. I wake up with my head on Jax's shoulder and find everyone else asleep as well. There's no telling if it's night or day in this tunnel. I'm honestly at a loss as to what to do. Do we go back to the village to find more help? Or is another angry mob waiting?

Suddenly I hear a clicking sound. I look up. The door is glowing bright orange.

"Everyone, wake up!" I nudge Jax and my parents. Jocelyn stretches her arms and yawns. "Look at the door! Someone is coming!"

"Everyone back. That door could blow," Father tells us.

We run into the tunnels just in time. The door blows open, and the tunnel fills with smoke, making everyone cough. When it clears, we can see through the opening to a brick wall on the other side. It's covered in pink roses. No one is there to greet us.

"Hello?" Maxine calls, her voice echoing off the walls.

There's no answer.

"What are you all waiting for?" Jocelyn asks. "This is our chance to get out of here." She runs for the opening.

As Jocelyn crosses the threshold, several flowers fly off

the walls and head right toward her. I realize too late that the stems are darts.

"Jocelyn, look out!" I shout, but she's already realized what's happening and ducked. The flower darts go flying over her head, heading toward the tunnel. "Drop!" I cry, and we fall to the ground as the darts whisk past us.

More darts come flying in our direction, followed by the sound of rumbling as the brick wall on the other side of the opening begins to come apart. I hear a loud whistle and watch in horror as the bricks begin flying toward us.

"We need to get out of here!" Jax shouts. "Forward!" He crawls on his elbows toward the opening and Jocelyn. "We'll face whatever is on the other side."

"Trixie, stay behind us," says Mother as more flower darts fly past our heads.

A brick smashes into the wall next to us, and the wall begins to crumble.

Trixie is crying again. Part of me wonders if we should tell her to head back into the tunnel for safety, but what if the doorway closes up and she's trapped? She has to come too. I follow Jax and the others into the opening and climb through to the other side. For a moment, the darts and bricks stop coming.

I look around. The sight of several cells with bars makes me think we're in the FTRS dungeon, but we could be in any dungeon for all I know. Just as I turn to look for some sort of landmark, more bricks shoot out of the wall. I roll to the right, and Jocelyn and Jax roll to the left. The bricks somehow follow us. I hear voices.

"Fire! Fire! Fire! We've been breached!" someone shouts.

"Get them! Show no mercy!"

"Defend our home at all costs!"

I hear cheers and hollering. Someone throws another smoke bomb and it explodes, shrouding the dungeon in darkness.

"Got one! Got two! Got three!"

I hear Trixie scream.

My family! What if it's the Stiltskin Squad? I reach for the mini wand in my pocket and realize I must have lost it. Arrows and bricks continue to fly as I look around for a weapon. I spy a whip hanging from the wall and grab it just as a dart hits me in the shoulder, piercing the skin.

"Ouch!" I shout and rip it out, but it's too late.

Immediately, I feel woozy. The room around me spins and goes out of focus as I struggle to hold on to the whip.

I give it a crack, sending arrows straight to the ground. I crack it again and blast a brick to smithereens. My strength is leaving me. I start to tumble. Someone is coming right at me.

"It's Gilly!" I hear them say right before the world goes dark.

CHAPTER 13

An Uncertain Future

"Y ou could have killed her!"

"But I didn't!"

"That's not the point!"

I hear arguing and open my eyes. The view is hazy, but I can tell I'm lying on a couch surrounded by a large group of people. Wilson's pink nose is nudging my chin.

"She's awake!" Madame Cleo is being broadcast from Blackbeard's mirror, which he is holding over me. "See? There was no need to worry, darlings. Gilly, dear, how are you?"

I open my mouth to speak, but my throat feels dry. All that comes out is gurgling.

Madame Cleo's hair turns blue. "Oh dear."

Slowly, they all come into view and I see my professors,

along with Headmistress Flora and my parents. My mother has a cold compress on my forehead, and Trixie is holding my hand. Jax has a cut on his forehead, and Jocelyn's got several scratches. Maxine's gray face is covered in black ash. Ollie and AG are here, too, and Ollie is wearing his Royal Lads-in-Waiting sash. The only one I don't see is Kayla.

I start to cough. "I'm okay," I choke out.

"The counterserum must be working. Otherwise she'd be dead right now." Professor Harlow glares at the person next to her. "What were you thinking, putting poison in those darts?"

A goblin girl wearing several pairs of earrings and a long, pink sash that says ROYAL LADIES-IN-WAITING crosses her arms. "You said defend the school at all costs! We were doing our job! Right, Tessa?"

The RLW's leader fiddles with several strands of pearls around her neck. "Well, um, yes? Which is why I took it upon myself to make some modifications to our weapons." Tessa narrows her eyes at me. "Raz taught us to be warriors! We defend our school at all costs even if she can't be here to guide us!" A cheer rises up from the RLWs in the room, including Ollie.

"Ollie, you attacked us too?" I ask incredulously.

He gulps hard. "I didn't know it was you guys."

"You almost killed a student!" Professor Sebastian roars. "Detention for all the RLWs—including the lad!" Tessa and Raza burst into tears. Ollie covers his face with his pirate bandanna.

I sit up slowly and Wilson runs down my arm. I place him back in my uniform pocket. "I'm okay. Really." I'm actually sort of impressed. Who knew the RLWs could be so rebellious?

Beauty puts her hand on Professor Sebastian's shoulder. "Gillian is fine. Now is no time for detention."

"I know, but Stiltskin's already made two wishes," Professor Sebastian says. "The Fire Moon is tonight. We're almost out of time!" He pounds the table I'm sitting on, and it cracks.

I hurry to get off it. "You mean one day away," I correct him.

"It's tonight," Harlow says. "You've been out cold for hours."

"*No!*" I cry. "How could you let me sleep that long?"

Pop! Pop! Pop! Merfolk appear in glass tanks around the

room. Headmistress Flora's door flies open, and a large group of students burst in. Most are wearing FTRS's blue uniforms, but some are in ball gowns and fancy blue velvet suits. The fancy-schmancies have silver sashes on over their outfits that say Royal Academy in sparkling letters. I recognize two girls in coordinating pink and purple gowns—Dahlia and Azalea, Flora's daughters (or, as some people still refer to them, "the Wicked Stepsisters." I've always found them pretty nice, if a tad obsessed with shopping.).

Flora embraces them. "You're all right! I was so worried."

"We're fine," Azalea says. "When Stiltskin took over the royal court with his wish about Gilly being a villain, we came as fast as we could. Well, first, we packed all our shoes—"

"And handbags," Azalea reminds her.

"But sadly, couldn't figure out how to bewitch our wardrobe closets to follow us," Dahlia says glumly, "and headed here. We invited all remaining RA kids to join us. That's what Princess Rose suggested we do before she went off to help Gilly." She looks at me. "Looks like she found you. At least one thing went right today."

Azalea shakes her head. "I really wish we could have brought that wardrobe closet."

"Now that you're all here, it's time for you to go," Professor Sebastian tells us. "You're going into hiding."

"What? Why?" Jocelyn asks.

"Children, it's our job to protect you," Beauty tells all the students. "This panic room is fully stocked and can fit all of you. We can take you there before Stiltskin arrives and maybe…" Her voice trails off. We all know even that room won't protect us from the curse.

"I'm sorry, but wasn't the whole point of FTRS to teach wicked delinquents and former villains how to turn into future heroes?" Maxine asks. There is a chorus of agreement around the room. "We aren't leaving. We are defending our school and our kingdom till the very end."

Robin Hood and Red burst through a trapdoor in the floor, knocking a few FTRS kids off balance. "Fair lady Flora," Robin says, "we are here to help! We have amassed forest friends and friendly giants like Erp. They await your orders at the edge of the school grounds."

Maxine grabs my arm. "Reinforcements! Our own army! This is good. Maybe we have a shot here!"

Flora looks at the assembled students. "Okay, then. If you're staying put, let's be clear: This is a battle to save not only our lives, but our world as we know it. If we lose, Enchantasia will be reborn in Stiltskin's vision. But if we stop this curse, we may be able to rid Enchantasia of Alva and Stiltskin forever." The assembled group cheers. "So let's make sure you're prepared, shall we?" Flora presses a button on her desk.

Boom! Boom! Boom!

Armored walls come down over every window in the headmistress's office. Portraits of our teachers hanging on the wall swing open, revealing hidden panels. The secret compartments light up, revealing an arsenal of weapons including magic wands, crossbows, potions, swords, bows and arrows, and rocks. I look at Headmistress Flora in awe.

"You've been away," she explains, grabbing a crossbow that she sprinkles with gingerroot, a substance that has helped us fight Alva before. "We've made a few modifications to the castle while you've been gone."

"I'll say," says Ollie, holding a shiny, new metal sword with glee.

"Everyone get a weapon," Flora tells the group, "then head to the gym to practice with them. And try to get some sleep. The Fire Moon is tonight. We will need all the time we can get to be ready."

Kids clamor to the cabinets, making a lot of noise as they argue over the merits of a huntsman's ax or a dagger that will head toward your target when you whisper their name. I grab a new bow and arrow. Jax takes a new sword. Jocelyn and Maxine take a sack full of potions that Peaches jumps inside.

"Be careful in the halls," Flora says as the students file out with Red and Robin taking the lead. "I sped up the hallway monitoring system for extra protection."

Madame Cleo appears in Blackbeard's mirror. "Blackbeard and I will head to the ship and take the merfolk and pirates with us. We will battle these foes from land and sea." There is more cheering (plus gurgling inside the tanks). People are definitely getting pumped up now.

Ollie puts a hand on my arm. "I think I can do more good on the ship, so I'm going to go with Blackbeard."

My face falls. I hate to see us separated. "Of course. Be careful out there, okay?" I feel my heart constrict slightly.

Ollie hugs me. "You too." He clinks swords with Jax before running off.

Harlow blocks the exit before Jocelyn, Maxine, Jax, and I can even consider where we belong.

"Uh-uh. Not you four." She points to me. "We've been

waiting for days to hear everything that has happened since we last spoke via mirror." She narrows her eyes. "And don't leave out a single detail."

When I'm finished talking, Harlow throws up her hands in exasperation.

"Our hope rests with a quorum? Quorums are almost unheard of!" Harlow says. "They require six fairies! The fairy students have already left school because they're so frightened of Alva." I open my mouth to respond, but Harlow already knows what I'm thinking. "You don't count." Harlow dismisses me with a wave of her hand. "You've never shown an ounce of fairy skill." Her raven, Argo, squawks in agreement.

"I'm working on it," I say and look at Father. "Grandma Pearl told me what to concentrate on. Maybe you could do the same," I say hopefully.

"I'm afraid I've suppressed my fairy side for too many years," he says. "I'd be of no help now." He holds Trixie close. "And I can't risk your sister, not after your brothers…"

"We don't have enough fairies to make this work." Headmistress Flora sighs.

"What about the harp pieces?" Maxine asks. "Did Madame Cleo find them?"

Professor Sebastian growls. "After several hypnosis sessions with Professor Harlow, it turns out Madame Cleo forgot she destroyed them."

"What?" Jocelyn cries.

Harlow rubs her temples, the stress of this incident obviously still getting to her. "She said she didn't want them falling into Stiltskin's hands, so she did what she thought was best."

"This is good news, right?" I say, grabbing a paperweight on Flora's desk and playing with it. "Now he can't cast the curse."

"Possibly," Wolfington says. "But if he needed the harp that badly, why didn't he use a wish to learn the truth? Instead he's been using his wishes to track you. It makes us wonder if he's found another way to cast his curse."

I feel my hope sink fast. I drop the paperweight on the desk. Peaches sees it, sticks her bill on the desk, and swallows it whole.

"Peaches!" Maxine scolds. "You give that back! It's the headmistress's!"

"*Quack!*" Peaches tells Maxine. "*Quack! Quack!*"

"Give it back!" Maxine says sternly.

Finally, Peaches begins to cough and regurgitate the paperweight. Seconds later, I see the slimy paperweight fall to the floor. It's the size of a quill now.

Maxine sighs. "I'm sorry, Professor. I'll buy you a new one." She looks at Peaches. "And I'm taking the money out of your allowance!" Peaches quacks again.

"It's all right," Flora says. "Why don't you take Peaches to get some real food so she stops eating things?" the headmistress suggests. "You should all eat something before... Well, just eat and get ready. Gillian will be along with her family shortly."

Jax and I look at each other as Maxine and Jocelyn head to the door. "See you later, thief."

"You can count on it," I say, but we both know nothing is certain. What if everyone is wrong, and Stiltskin shows up now? I watch them go as Angelina rushes in behind them with Kayla and her two sisters. She's holding the book containing Rumpelstiltskin's story in her hands.

"Flora!" she says. "The book has changed again." She sees me and breathes a sigh of relief. "Gilly, I'm glad you're here. This concerns you too."

"What's changed now?" Harlow says with exasperation.

"This could help us." Angelina places the book on Flora's desk. "Stiltskin thinks once the book is finished, it's complete, but the truth is his story won't be over till he's gone. His story will continue to change based on what happens in the present. When Anna took Gilly's brothers, his story shifted again. I still see the curse being cast, but its results are cloudy now. Certainly not as concrete as they were before. This is good! Alva is angry at Stiltskin! Perhaps it's because Alva can be impulsive," she tells the teachers, and I think of how Grandma Pearl said the same thing. "She's angry Stiltskin hasn't gotten his hands on Gilly. The boys aren't what they wanted, but they will use them for bait. But so far, you haven't gone to him."

"Because I've been knocked out cold here," I explain.

"He doesn't know that. All he knows is you aren't coming. That means he has to come to you. Alva hates making the first move," Angelina explains. "She becomes frustrated when things don't go exactly her way, which I don't believe they will. That gives us a chance."

"If he's coming, we need to do something about securing the other Cobblers," Harlow says. "Stiltskin's already taken two. We can't let him nab the rest."

"That's true." Flora thinks for a moment. "Mr. and Mrs. Cobbler, have you ever taken fairy shrinking potion? Angelina's fairy house might be the safest spot to hold you for now."

Father groans. "As a child. It gives me a headache." Mother clears her throat. "But we will do whatever you need us to do." He looks at me. "Gillian, you'll come too?"

"No," I say before Flora can answer for me. "I'm the only one that might have a chance at getting Anna to give me back the boys. I have to try." I can't let something happen to Trixie. If Father and Mother go with her, at least I know they'll all be safe.

"My daughters Brook Lynn and Emma Rose will bring you to the fairy house and help you get settled," Angelina tells them. "I will be back as soon as I can." She looks at me. "I need to speak to Gilly first."

Trixie and Father hug me. Father whispers in my ear. "If Anna will listen to anyone, it's you. Be safe, my brave girl."

"I will," I tell him.

"You're more powerful than you realize," Mother adds. "When the time comes, trust your heart. It won't lead you astray."

"But what if what my heart wants and what I should

actually do are different things?" I ask, thinking of Anna. "No matter how hard I try, I can't make everyone happy."

Mother laughs. "Dear girl, no one can. You can't force people to see differently, even if you believe they're making the wrong choice." She looks into my eyes. "They need to see the truth on their own. Do what's right for you in that moment. I know you'll be all right."

"I will." But as I watch them leave Flora's office with Brook Lynn and Emma Rose, I can't help but wonder: Is this the last time I'll see my family?

Angelina takes my hand. Kayla flutters beside her. "Now we get to work helping you find your inner fairy."

"It won't work," I say. "I've tried. Ask Kayla. And I need full abilities for me to help form a quorum."

"Night hasn't fallen yet," Angelina says. "Whatever Stiltskin has planned, he can't make it happen till the Fire Moon is upon us."

"And let's not forget, he never wants to fight unless he has to," Professor Sebastian says. "He'd rather make a deal. They're his favorite thing in the world. When he arrives—and he will—you cannot give in to him. No matter what happens, Gillian."

"Use one of the classrooms to practice," Flora says as Angelina and Kayla lead me out of the room. "It will be quieter. I'll check in later."

I work with Angelina and Kayla for hours, practicing mindfulness and the art of being in tune with nature (which involves a lot of me in the garden talking to the pumpkin patch).

"A lot of fairy behavior is a feeling," Angelina says when I fail to diagnose a plant in desperate need of water.

Outside the window, I see the glow of the sky changing colors. Night is falling. My stomach twists anxiously at the thought. "What I'm feeling right now is anxious," I admit.

"Listen to the feeling! Go with your gut and your instincts." She takes my hand. "But above all else, believe in yourself. If you truly believe you are a fairy, which you are, you will be one. I'm going to go check on your parents and Trixie. Maybe I can work them, too, before it's time. If we need that quorum…" She trails off.

She doesn't need to continue the thought. I know what she is thinking: if we need a quorum, and we don't have six fairies, we won't be able to stop Stiltskin.

"Keep working with Kayla," Angelina adds with a smile, and she touches my cheek. "I have faith in you, Gilly."

"Thank you," I say. I just wish I had faith in myself.

Kayla and I work so long that eventually we both fall asleep at the table. We're awoken hours later by the sound of a siren.

"Warning! Intruder approaching!" a voice blares as the warning siren screams throughout the castle, waking Kayla and me up.

The mirrors in the room come alive, the glass turning bright red. Miri the Magic Mirror roars to life. "Rumpelstiltskin! He's here!"

CHAPTER 14

The Beginning of the End

The lanterns in the classroom suddenly extinguish, plunging us into darkness. Miri's mirrors cut out. I hear screaming in the distance as a rumble rocks the castle.

"We need to get out of here and see what's going on," I tell Kayla.

The door to the classroom flies open.

"Thief? Kayla? Are you guys all right?" Jax lights a flare so we can see one another. Maxine is with him.

Quack!

So is Peaches.

"What is going on? Where is Miri?" Kayla asks.

Ah-woooo! We hear a wolf howl somewhere close by.

"Stiltskin must have knocked out our magic mirror

system and the castle torches. We can't tell what's going on," Jax explains. "Wolfington, Professor Sebastian, and AG will be transforming in Flora's office. We do not want to be here when they do," he says. "Flora has most of the students in the gym awaiting instruction while Jocelyn and Harlow try to hold up the barrier. We can meet them there."

"I need to find my mother," Kayla tells me, and her wings pop out and begin to flutter.

"Wait!" I say as she flies off. "Shouldn't we stay together?"

"We need more fairies!" she yells as she flies into the hallway. "I'll find you!"

I'm not alone, I remind myself, but our group size is dwindling. Another blast sends pieces of the ceiling crumbling down on us. I look up and see a small hole in the ceiling, revealing a red sky.

The Fire Moon is here.

"We need to get outside," I tell Jax.

"The Magical Fairy Pets classroom is in this hallway," Maxine tells us. "It has a back door."

The three of us, with Peaches in tow, rush down the hall and into the classroom. A lion roars in greeting. Cages with fairy pets big and small, with everything from elephants to tigers and peacocks, are locked inside them. Another blast rocks the castle, and the sound of the animals' combined calls for help is deafening.

"We have to release them. They're goners if we don't," Maxine runs from cage to cage to open them up. An elephant runs past me, and Jax and I press ourselves against a wall to avoid being trampled. The animal crashes right through the wall, giving us a view of the outside world.

The sky is smoky, lit entirely by the red glow of the Fire Moon. I watch as a cannonball blasts into the air, lighting up the cornfields and the forest below. A low-lying fog is seeping out from the trees, which rattle with the appearance of several giants. Overhead, gargoyles fly in front of the moon, followed by harpies whose shrieks are so loud, the fairy pets wail louder with fright. Finally, a large group emerges out of the darkness: Stiltskin and Alva are leading the crowd to the protective shield crackling around the school.

Stiltskin is dressed entirely in gold, and his black beard has only grown longer in his time away. Still, it's my first sighting of Alva that makes me the most anxious. When we saw her in Cloud City, she was still unconscious after I unwittingly released her from her statue prison. Now Alva's jet-black hair flies untamed in the wind as she holds up a wand and points it at the shield, lighting it up like a thousand fairies. The massive Stiltskin Squad watches her in awe. Standing front and center, watching, is my sister, Anna.

I'm not sure you can save that one, I hear Grandma Pearl say inside my head, but I try to block her out and focus on Angelina's instructions: *What does your gut tell you?*

That my sister is a villain now. I know this to be true. But if faced with a choice, will I have what it takes to destroy Anna to save the kingdom? Can I handle how evil she's truly become and accept I can't save her?

For the first time in a long time, I'm scared.

"Come out, come out, wherever you are!" Alva's voice echoes through the room like a gust of wind. "I know you've got the girl."

I know she means me.

"You think you can hide behind shields that can't be broken, but we will get inside!" Her laugh bounces off the walls. "Give us what we came for, and there is a chance some of you may be spared."

"You're not surrendering," Jax tells me. "Don't even think of it."

"I know, but if she destroys the school to get to me, so many lives will be lost. I can't let that happen either." I try to control my breathing like Angelina taught me and not be rash. *Don't rush*, I hear a voice inside my head say. *Make them wait for you.*

"Why won't they come?" Stiltskin hops up and down angrily. "Cowards!" I'm not sure he realizes his tinny voice is picked up by Alva's magical speaker spell. It echoes through the castle. "We need to get that shield down!"

"I'm trying!" Alva barks as she lights the barricade again using her wand fire. The shield, however, stays intact. Alva finally throws her wand, frustrated.

"They're trying to stall us!" Stiltskin shouts. "I know that angers you, but remain calm. I want our future here already, too, my pet." He takes her hand.

Ugh. My pet? That's just the worst nickname ever.

"They're scared." Alva pulls her hand away. "Good! Let them cower!" She takes a deep breath. "Their fear feeds my soul. You're afraid to leave the security of your castle, are you?" she shouts and her voice swooshes through the room. "Well, you'll want to leave when you see who is coming for you."

"I should show myself," I say and I hear the voice again. *Be patient.* So instead, I stay still, watching Alva's every move.

Suddenly there is a plume of smoke and flames and Alva transforms herself into a wyvern. The two-headed dragon nearly destroyed the royal court the last time Alva managed this feat. But this time, the damage could be worse. The wyvern takes flight, its wings beating fast as it inhales sharply, then emits a long stream of fire at the barricade protecting the school. This time, the shield sizzles and cracks, sounding like fireworks before it finally explodes. Jax and I reach for each other as the holes in the shield grow larger and larger until it completely disintegrates. Within seconds, Stiltskin and his crew begin running straight toward the school.

"We need to move!" Jax says, pulling me back from the opening. I reach for Maxine.

"But the animals!" Maxine cries. "I have to free the rest of them, or they'll have no chance."

"Maxine—" I try, but she cuts me off as the wyvern sets the nearby greenhouse ablaze.

"No." Her jaw is firm. "I must do this, Gilly. Please."

"But…" I hesitate, but I know what Angelina would say: Everyone has their own path. I nod reluctantly. "Be careful."

"I will." Maxine looks at Jax. "Get Gilly somewhere safe. I'll come find you." Maxine sets a unicorn free, and it jumps through the hole in the wall.

Jax grabs my arm again, and I feel Wilson scurry out of my pocket and down my arm.

There is so much commotion and noise I can barely understand what he's squeaking, but I assume it's about him staying back as well. *Everyone needs their own path.* I take a deep breath. "Okay, but come with Peaches as soon as you're done. Promise you'll find us!" I shout to Maxine, but I can barely see her through all the smoke. I feel Jax reach for my hand again.

"Let's get you to the fairy grounds! You need to get to Angelina!" he shouts, and we tear off into the field.

CHAPTER 15

Darkness before the Light

The Fire Moon is high in the sky when Jax and I take off across the field. I hang on to Jax's hand as we run, aghast at the scenes unfolding right in front of us. The ground continues to quake from the explosions and the footsteps of giants.

I see Jack chasing down two giants on Stiltskin's squad from high atop Erp's back. *BAM!* He throws something at the back of a giant, and I watch as the explosion produces an ivy vine that twists up and around one of the giant's legs, knocking him to the ground.

In the lake in the distance, pirates are battling Stiltskin Squad members on the deck, while cannon fire booms off the side of the ship. I can't see Ollie, but I imagine him there, fighting with all his might.

Fireballs shoot by us, lighting the cornfields on fire, and I wonder if they're coming from Jocelyn. There is a loud cheer as some of the Stiltskin Squad go running toward the woods at the sight of flames.

There is so much smoke and ash that I am not even sure of my surroundings. If Jax weren't with me, I'm not even sure which way I'd go. The fairy gardens seem very far away.

"I need to find my brothers," I shout.

"Nothing is going to happen to them," he insists. "Stiltskin needs them alive to get you to come to him. Angelina told you to come to her when the battle begins, remember? Focus on getting a quorum."

Whoosh! My hair blows all around me as one of Robin's arrows whizzes by us with Robin in tow. He hangs on by one arm, aiming his arrows from his quiver in the other. Red is right behind him, firing arrow after arrow.

"Gilly!" she shouts. "We spotted your brothers! They're being held in the woods just beyond the cornfields. We are headed there! Follow us!"

I feel a glimmer of hope, which pops fast when I see Gretel is gaining on Red. She's riding on a bewitched flying cast-iron skillet, trying to catch her. I let go of Jax's hand and start running toward Red. "Watch out!" I shout.

I hear a scream and whirl around. Hansel has grabbed Jax from high atop his own flying skillet. Jax dangles precariously by one arm as Hansel races away with him in tow.

"Gilly!" Jax shouts.

I turn back. "Hang on!" I yell as I race after Hansel, who is headed in the opposite direction.

Spotting a massive pumpkin in the patch in front of me, I jump onto it and launch myself into the air. My hand manages to close on one of Jax's legs as Hansel and his skillet continue to climb. The weight of two added passengers slows down the cast-iron skillet a great deal. The cookware begins to zoom downward, headed for a line of trees.

"Let go! We're going to crash!" Hansel tries to shake Jax free, but Jax hangs on for dear life, and I hang on to Jax. The skillet starts to spin and sputter, but jumping at this speed would be foolish. We're tumbling so fast, I can't make out the sky from the ground. Hansel's cookware hits a tree, and he goes flying, pulling us along with him.

Jax and I are thrown backward, crashing into a bush. For a moment, all is silent, and there's a ringing in my ears. When

I sit up, I have a gash on my arm, and my head is throbbing. Standing is difficult, but I hold on to the tree as I pull myself up. Someone reaches out and grabs my ankle.

"Thief, grabbing on to that skillet was a risky move." Jax jokes, but his voice is weak and he looks pale.

"Maybe, but we need to look out for each other." I help him up and look around. We are nowhere near Angelina's fairy garden now. We're actually on the outskirts of the woods. I spot what's left of Hansel's skillet beside a smoking tree. Hansel lies motionless next to it, but there is no time to check on him. I hear footsteps and quickly pull Jax behind a tree.

Anna has Han and Hamish by the hand and is running our way. I don't hesitate. I jump into her path and pull an arrow from my pack, aiming it at her heart. She freezes in her tracks.

"Boys!" I yell. "Step back!"

"Gilly!" Han cries, gulping so hard he can't even breathe. "We can't!" He holds up his small hand, and I see a glowing cuff attaching him to Hamish and Anna. "She won't let us go."

"Something's wrong with Anna!" Hamish adds, sobbing harder. "Do something!"

I keep the arrow trained on her. Anna's eyes are as black as coal, as if she's under a spell. "Let them go."

"Gilly, don't be a fool," she hisses. "Just listen to—"

I let the arrow go. It narrowly misses her shoulder on purpose. She blinks in surprise, and so do I. I had her, and again, I couldn't do what I probably should have. "No, *you* listen!" I shout as Jax stands weaponless beside me. "These are your brothers! Give them to me, and I'll let you go back to Stiltskin. He's the only one you care about anymore."

The darkness in Anna's eyes flickers and fades for a moment. "No, I..."

But her words disappear as a sudden blast hits Jax in the chest, sending him flying. I scream and run toward him. He's been knocked unconscious. When I look up, I see Gretel emerging from the trees, pointing a wand right at me and Jax.

"Good work—you got her!" Gretel says to Anna. "Cuff her with the boys."

Anna hesitates, looking as scared of me as I was of facing her. Then she heads toward me to do as she's told.

And that's when something starts to bubble up inside me. It's a feeling rising to the surface that I can't squash down anymore even if I want to. *Forget Anna! Save the boys! They're innocent!* the voice shouts, and that's when I realize, finally, that the inner voice is actually my own, and I'm ready to listen. The vial attached to the strand of pearls on my neck start to glow.

"What is that?" Gretel asks, looking at my necklace.

Instinctively, I snap the vial off the necklace and toss it toward her. Seconds later, the vial explodes, immobilizing Gretel and Anna. I'm not sure how long the magic will hold, so I don't hesitate. I reach forward, snatching the key around Anna's neck, which I use to free Han and Hamish. The moment they're free, I rush back to Jax. Jax groans when I pull him up to standing and place his arm around my shoulder. "Boys, we don't have much time! Help me hold him. We need to run!" I take two steps forward with him, and we both stumble.

"Thief?" His voice is weak. I see a hole in his uniform shirt near his right shoulder. He's bleeding. "You have to get the boys somewhere safe. Go."

"No," I insist. "We're all going together. Come on. You can make it." I try to pull him forward again, and that's when I hear the crackling sound.

Wand fire is coming straight for us. Han screams, but there is no time to even react. I pull the others close and brace for impact.

Pop! A red bubble appears around me, Jax, and the boys, like our own small shield. Grandma Pearl has come through again. The wand fire bounces off the shield instead and hits a nearby tree, which is quickly engulfed by flames.

"No!" Gretel shouts. "Get that shield down!"

"I can't let you have them, Gilly!" Anna says, walking toward the shield. "You're all coming with me."

"I don't think so." I look around for a clear path out of the fire, hoping the bubble will move with me, much like the one we were in when Grandma Pearl attempted to send us back to FTRS, but the smoke is expanding, and it's hard to see anything. Finally, I spot a small opening in the trees. I slowly move us and the bubble toward it.

Anna and Gretel both fire again and again, but the bubble holds firm. The wand fire continues to ricochet off it until I hear a scream and realize one of the sparks has ricocheted and hit Anna in her boot.

"Pay attention!" Gretel shouts. "They're getting away!"

We're almost there. I can see the battle on the field through the trees. Outside the forest there will be allies, someone to help Jax, reinforcements. We just need to keep moving. Almost there... We burst through the last batch of trees into the smoke and ashy sky and stumble right into his Stiltskin himself.

"Where do you think you're going, Gillian Cobbler?" he asks, a sick smile on his lips. I notice the magic lamp is hooked on Stiltskin's sheath, close to his side. Stiltskin Squad members crowd around the bubble from all sides.

We're still too far from the main battle for anyone to realize we're in jeopardy. Jax is too weak to run any farther, and the boys are too small to make any quick moves. We are surrounded by Stiltskin's crew, the wyvern has taken flight and is headed our way, and I don't see our friends anywhere. My worst fear has come true: I'm truly alone.

He steps forward to touch the bubble and it singes his fingers. He holds his flaming-red hand in horror. "What is that thing? Anna? Gretel! Get it down! Now!"

"We're trying!" Gretel says, racing up behind us again and hitting the bubble with more wand fire. It ricochets and almost hits two Stiltskin Squad members, who dive for cover.

"Gilly, please," Anna begs. "Drop your shield. You don't

understand. We are on the same side! Stiltskin is going to protect us in his curse."

"No, you don't understand, Anna!" I try to hold Jax up by one arm, and the boys cling to my other one. "Look around. Does this look like he's protecting us? He wants to destroy everything we love!"

"Everything *you* love!" My little sister's face contorts with anger. "I want to start over. I want the chance to be great! Like you are! But in this world, you took all the glory and left me with nothing!"

Stiltskin's laugh pierces through our argument. "Getting along as well as always, I see. Anna, are you sure you want to keep her around when Enchantasia is reborn? I was thinking maybe—"

A fireball comes sailing overhead and lands in front of him, knocking him off his feet. Another fires right after it and then another. Stiltskin Squad members run for cover. Through the smoke and the ash, I spot two sisters racing toward me—Professor Harlow and Jocelyn. They aim again and again in unison, singeing the trees around Stiltskin and his squad. Gretel gets hit in the leg and limps off in pain. Anna retreats, and Stiltskin hides behind some rocks, where something on his sheath bursts, sending what look like beads flying everywhere.

For a moment, I think we've got him, but then I see the wyvern blanket the ground behind Harlow and Jocelyn with fire. My friends quickly put up a shield to protect themselves while the ground around us is turned to charred ash.

Come on, Grandma Pearl! I will the bubble, focusing on what I really need. *Get us out of here. Let me get the boys somewhere safe!*

"We *are* safe, Gilly," Han tells me. "We're with you."

I look at them. "I didn't say that out loud," I say. "Did I?" Jax drifts in and out, unable to answer me.

The wyvern roars louder in frustration, and I watch as the beast crackles and glows bright red before wavering in front of our eyes. Once more, a woman stands in our midst.

"Harlow, old friend, so we meet again." Alva strides toward Harlow's bubble and pierces it with a simple wave of the wand in her hand. "I never had a chance to thank you for all you did the last time I visited the school." She aims her wand at Jocelyn, and I inhale sharply.

Jocelyn and I make eye contact for the briefest of moments

before Harlow waves her wand again, sending the bubble Jocelyn is in into the air, where it disappears from sight.

Alva laughs. "Clever. Saving the girl. But it won't save you."

"Maybe not," Harlow says calmly. "But I'll get my joy while I can. I'm still quite fond of the time I got to watch you become encased in stone."

"You'll pay for that move." Alva raises her wand again.

Harlow and Alva aim their wands at each other, sending streaks of electricity into the air. The remaining Stiltskin Squad members watch, mesmerized by the battle.

Jax starts to slip, and I try to hold him up. "Jax! Wake up!" I say. "We have to get out of here."

"Gilly?" Han's eyes widen. "Is he dying?"

"No!" I insist. "We just have to get him help."

Harlow has them distracted for now, but how do I get help when I'm surrounded? I hear Alva scream and look up. Harlow is gaining on her. Harlow pushes her wand stream harder, and Alva begins to sink into the ground from the pressure.

"No!" Stiltskin races out of his hole and throws a magic bean onto the ground. A vortex opens up below Harlow's feet.

"Don't!" Alva cries at the same time I do.

"Gillian! Look at me!" Harlow says as the world around

her starts to spin. "Your biggest enemy has always been your-self. You are bigger than your fears!" she shouts as the wind pulls her into its spiral and down into the vortex. "Do what you have to do to fig—"

"NO!" I reach out, but she's already gone.

Alva lets out a bloodcurdling scream, startling me. "You two-foot tyrant!" She storms over to Stiltskin and blasts the ground in front of him. "You let your anger control you, and now we've lost Harlow! She could have been a powerful aid with this curse. I could have swayed her!"

"My pet, I was trying to save you!" Stiltskin looks at the Wicked Fairy with such googly eyes I feel ill. "She almost had you done for! I couldn't survive without you again."

Alva is his weakness. Isn't that what Angelina once said? I listen carefully as gargoyles fly in from all directions, sur-rounding my bubble. I pull everyone in closer.

"Jax?" I nudge him as the boys cry softly into my side. "I could really use some help here." But he drifts in and out of consciousness. I look around frantically for the others, wondering where Angelina is. Has Kayla found her? What am I supposed to do? Who knows where our friends are or if they're even alive?

"I wouldn't have let her. I still had fight in me!" Alva rails against him, and some of the Stiltskin Squad back away nervously. "Now who knows where your bean sent her? We'll never get her back in time for the curse to be cast!"

"We don't need her, my pet," Stiltskin says, but his eyes are flitting wildly. "We have plenty of dark souls on our side. Like Anna!" He motions to my sister.

"Oh, Anna!" Alva laughs. "You have such faith in a confused child! This one will not help you when it's time for the curse! You've trusted all these *children* for nothing! They're too young to see the greater good in what we hope to achieve."

"She will!" Stiltskin insists. "My squad is loyal! They know that what we're creating benefits all of us."

"Do they?" Alva says quietly. "The curse only works for the two of us, as you know." She glances at the anxious crowd behind them. "Did you ever tell them that?"

"What is she talking about?" Anna asks. "You said we'd be protected."

"You will be!" Stiltskin says as the grumbling grows louder. "You can all trust me! We're going to a new Enchantasia!"

But Anna is looking at him strangely now too. "If only

one other person can be part of the curse, how will my family be spared? I've held on to the boys because you assured me we'd all be okay. Will we?"

"I…" Stiltskin side-eyes Alva. "I hope so! Oh, don't look disappointed in me. I would have figured it out! I was going to make some modifications to our curse once I spoke to my pet. She wants me with her in this new world, of course, so I'd make sure you were there too. I never would have spilled your blood for the curse, Anna. Trust me on that. You've been faithful."

Anna begins to back away. "Spilled my blood?" Her face is pale.

Alva laughs. "Oh, darling, you didn't really think you could trust a villain, did you?" She looks toward my bubble. "I'm done playing games. The Fire Moon is high in the sky. We have all the ingredients we need right here. This curse begins now."

"You don't have the harp!" I stall, hearing my voice echo in the bubble. "And you never will! It's been destroyed!"

Alva starts to laugh wildly again. "Oh, child, you fool. We don't need the harp. We already have all we need—this moon, this place, high on a hilltop closer to the celestial sky."

She pulls out the golden egg I procured for Stiltskin, and I feel the color drain from my face. "This egg and fairy blood. And for that, I've always wanted yours. After all you've put me through, using your blood to enact this curse makes it all the more thrilling."

My blood. I feel the bubble start to waver. The power of Grandma Pearl's shield is fading. I pull everyone tighter to my side, looking frantically for Maxine, Jocelyn, or Kayla and her mother. I wonder where Ollie is at that exact moment. I feel my breath quicken and try to slow it down, remembering what Angelina taught me; what Harlow wanted me to remember: that I'm stronger than my fear. But the bubble is fading. I watch helplessly as it finally fades away.

CHAPTER 16

Truly Cursed

I reach for my quiver, but the gargoyles surrounding us are too fast. They rip Han and Hamish from me and fly them straight to Alva.

"Gilly! Help!" Han screams as Jax goes limp.

I hang on to him the best I can, but I have to let go if I'm going to save the boys. *Hang on!* a voice inside my head says. My heart is pounding as I make my choice. Jax goes down fast, crumpling by my feet. The gargoyles see him fall and screech louder. I pull an arrow from my quiver and nock it back.

"Touch them, and I'll strike you in your heart," I say, shaking.

Alva grins wickedly as she holds both boys by their shirts. "I like that fire in you, girl. Your sister could use some of that."

"Please! Don't hurt them," Anna begs Alva and Stiltskin. "You said nothing about using my family's fairy blood!"

"Well, whose did you think we'd use for the curse?" Alva asks as Stiltskin look guilty. "It never would have been mine. I always wanted Gillian's, but when we didn't catch her, I suggested you." She sighs. "Sadly, he's so fond of his star pupil that he said it had to be another fairy's. Someone truly good and heroic—which isn't you. That's your sister." She looks at me. "But if she won't sacrifice herself, then I guess one of her brothers will do. They're young and surely pure of heart." Her eyes flash. "Or maybe I should just use them both...to be sure." The boys' eyes widen in horror.

"No! Please!" Anna begs. "Not my brothers."

"Then tell your sister to sacrifice herself without any more fighting," Alva says calmly. "Then I'll let the boys go to live their last moments before the curse. I'm certainly not saving your family," she says with a small laugh. "The Cobblers have always gotten in the way of what I've done."

Alva places the egg on a rock in front of her, and my heart pounds wildly. What am I going to do?

"With Gillian's blood spilled, I will use Pearl's bloodline to finally end this. After all, this curse feeds on our feelings and our emotions, and hate is the strongest emotion of all. So Gillian, who will it be? Your brothers' blood or yours?" I open my mouth to respond. "Never mind. I hate waiting." Alva pulls a dagger from inside her dress and cuts the boys' palms in quick succession.

"No!" I let go of the arrow, and it sails toward Alva. She deflects it with a wave of her wrist. She turns their wrists so their blood drips onto the egg. It immediately starts to glow.

The curse has begun.

"Stop!" Anna begs. "Stiltskin, do something!"

"Gilly! Please!" Hamish yells.

"Someone help me!" I fire again and again, but the arrows bounce off Alva. Gargoyles swoop toward me and Jax lying at my feet. I feel no pity as I fire at them again and again, but they keep coming. I have no radishes on me now.

"Hang on!" I try not to cry as a gargoyle picks me up and holds me by the shirt. Another grabs Jax, who can barely hold his head up. I struggle to get out of its grasp. "Anna! Please! Stop this! They're your brothers!"

"It was Gilly or you, Anna," I hear Stiltskin say, and he actually looks somewhat apologetic. "Alva wouldn't settle for anyone but a Cobbler." Anna looks gobsmacked, and her chest starts to heave. "But don't you see? You don't need any of them anymore! We are your family now!"

The egg is blinding as it lights up the darkness of the forest, shooting a beam up at the Fire Moon before shooting across the sky, washing the clouds in a red glow. The wind kicks up and trees start to blow. Lightning hits a tree in the distance, and the tree explodes, cracking into a million pieces. The thunder rumbles continuously as the ground starts to shake, knocking me and the others to the ground.

"It's starting!" Stiltskin says with glee as Alva watches in amazement. "Enchantasia will be reborn, and we all will benefit from it!"

The light washes over the Pegasus stables at FTRS. They disappear in front of my eyes.

He's erasing us. He's going to erase everything. I try advancing on Alva to grab the boys, firing the last of my arrows at the egg, but it does nothing. The gargoyles surrounding me yank the quiver off my back as I look for a weapon of any kind to use, but I don't see any. I search Jax's pockets, but they too have nothing.

Please, Grandma Pearl. Please. What do I do? I beg, but there is no answer as I hang in the air unable to break free.

Think, Gilly! Think! It can't be too late. Even if I am alone. I am stronger than my fear. *Focus on your instincts*, I remind myself. *The lamp is the key.* The word comes to me so quickly I'm surprised. I glance at Stiltskin's lamp on the ground. *If I got it, could I force Darlene to let me be her master so I could stop this?* Desperate, I kick out from the gargoyle's grasp and fall to the ground. I lunge for the lamp.

"Uh, uh, uh!" Stiltskin grabs the lamp before I can reach it. The gargoyle grabs me again. "This isn't yours! You're always taking things that don't belong to you!"

The egg's rays touch the vegetable patch, and it dissolves. Next, the lake begins to get sucked up and Blackbeard's pirate ship along with it. Lightning crackles across the sky as the earth begins to split open beneath my feet. I can see people running in the distance, but there is nowhere to hide from this curse. The edges of the forest near school begin to drift away into the wind. I imagine my village and school getting sucked away. As more and more of the kingdom is sucked up, even the Stiltskin Squad looks anxious.

"Why isn't this curse working faster?" Alva continues to hold my brothers' hands over the egg. The boys have stopped crying now. They're just standing there in shock.

"Gilly, please…" Han says again, but his voice is fading.

"Please!" I shout. "The curse is working. You've won. Let my brothers go."

Alva only smiles up at me. "Never. Watching you suffer is part of the fun."

I hear a crack and watch as more and more of the forest disappears. A few giants get pulled up too and fade away.

Gretel grabs Stiltskin's gold lapel. "How do we keep from being sucked away?"

"You don't," Alva says.

"My pet, see reason! I've told you over and over that I won't leave without my squad and Anna."

"I see no use for any of them in our new world," Alva says dismissively. "Especially since you won't be in it either."

"I… What do you mean?" Stiltskin sputters.

Alva drops the dagger from her free hand and pulls out her wand. She whisks Darlene's lamp out of Stiltskin's hands and pulls it toward herself.

"What are you doing?" Stiltskin asks, his voice going up an octave. "My pet!"

"Don't call me your pet." Alva rolls her eyes. "I told you I hated that years ago!" She rubs the lamp. "I wish…" she says, and Darlene oozes out of her lamp again. She surveys the scene and gasps in horror. "I wish for you to banish Rumpelstiltskin to another realm from which he cannot return."

"What? No! You can't! My pet! No!" Stiltskin screams.

"I am your co-master, am I not?" Alva says coolly. "He made you make me one. Because he loves me." She smiles nastily.

And that's when Stiltskin realizes the truth at the same time I do: he's been beaten at his own game.

"Stop her!" he yells to his squad. "Stop her!"

But instead, they take this as their chance to run from the Wicked Fairy before this curse swallows them up whole. Anna is the only one who stays, her eyes on our brothers as Stiltskin runs for the lamp to knock it out of Alva's hands. But it's too late.

Darlene looks from Alva up to me. "Well...it's sort of an evil wish, which I despise, but your last wish wasn't much better, and I was forced to grant that, so..." Darlene smiles. "I guess I'll take the punishment from the genie council and be done with you!" She looks at Alva again. "As you wish," Darlene says.

Stiltskin screams. "No!"

Alva doesn't flinch.

Darlene closes her eyes, mumbles a few words, and there is a large gust of wind. I watch as it sucks the evil tyrant who caused us so much pain up into a vortex of wind. Alva and Anna watch it happen, and I take my chance. I try to pull Jax up to standing again and stagger toward the boys. Alva turns toward me and fires her wand. Jax and I get knocked onto our backs. My right shoulder is throbbing. I'm not even sure I can stand again.

"Alva, nooooo!" Stiltskin cries.

But his biggest weakness, the love of his life, watches quietly, not shedding a tear.

The funnel spins faster till it explodes with a pop and Stiltskin disappears into the light. There is complete silence as Darlene oozes back into her lamp, her work for Alva finally complete. The lamp clangs to the ground.

Anna is breathing hard. "Why did you do that to him?" she asks, and I know she's trying not to cry. "You loved him! He loved you!"

"Love is for fools," Alva says simply.

But I know she's wrong. Love is what's right in this kingdom, and no matter how much pain I'm in, I can't be like

Grandma Pearl and just give up. I can't be my own worst enemy and be afraid. I need to fight for the things I love, even if I die trying—and I just might. I take a deep breath and roll onto my side.

"Come on, Jax," I yell and he looks over at me. "We can get out of this. If this is the end, we need to make it count."

He smiles weakly and nods to the trees. "We will. Look."

I look over, and I could almost cry in relief. I'm not alone. Kayla, Jocelyn, Ollie, and Maxine are quietly racing up the hill!

"Fire!" I hear someone scream and look up to see Jack riding Erp through the trees. He drops smoke bombs onto the area as more kids come streaming out of the trees. Ollie, Maxine, and Jocelyn come running now too, shooting radishes into the air with small slingshots. Gargoyles begin falling from the sky. Angelina and Kayla's sisters are flying our way too. My parents and Trixie are flying with them, holding on to their backs.

Alva is so surprised that she doesn't see Peaches emerge from the trees, grab the lamp, and swallow it. When Peaches coughs it up seconds later, the lamp is small enough to fit into her beak. She picks it up and waddles back into the trees.

The gargoyles holding Jax and I even look fearful. Panicked, they drop Jax and me to the ground. Alva spins around, shocked to see her numbers dwindling. Still, she clings to the two boys. She looks at me.

"You may think this helps your cause, but look! Your school is fading away! Your village is gone! And soon you will be too." She presses a dagger to Hamish's neck, and my mother screams. "But not before I watch you suffer."

"No!" I reach out to stop her, but I'm stopped by the sound of an explosion. I look over to see where it came from and spot Jax, his arm still raised from whatever he's thrown at the ground. There is now a giant hole in the ground the size of a small house. It's a magic bean!

With sudden strength, I watch as Jax dives at Han and Hamish and pulls my brothers into the portal. I cry out. They're going to make it! They're going to get away!

But then I hear the blast of Alva's wand, which is aimed straight at Jax's heart.

"No!" I cry as the portal closes up tight. The wind that follows knocks everyone off their feet and the battle grinds to a halt, everyone standing where they are in stunned silence. My mother bursts into tears. I breathe heavily. Did Alva hit them, or did they get away just in time? Is Jax dead? I feel a pain rip at my insides like I've never felt before. All I want to do is roll over and die.

"You killed them." Anna's voice is hollow.

"What's done is done," Alva says firmly. "You're still here. I'm still here. Want to know why? We're survivors! And now, we can finish this. We can hasten the curse's effects, and Enchantasia will be reborn. Together we will win all we've ever wanted."

"But you said…" Anna starts to say, tears falling down her cheeks.

"I can say anything I want," Alva tells her. "It's my curse and you've proven to be a better ally than I could have imagined. Now, you can join me."

In the distance, I see FTRS start to be sucked into the nothingness. The girls' and boys' dormitory turrets disappear from view forevermore. My brothers are lost. My teachers have disappeared. Jax is gone. Soon there will be nothing left. *Unless…* The thought is roaring to the surface, begging to be heard. *We can still win.*

I look to Angelina, who is consoling my mother. "We have to try to create a quorum," I say as Alva continues to corral my sister.

"But we don't have enough fairies," Angelina says as she holds my mother close. "The girls and I only make four."

"And I make four and a half," I say. "Maybe it's not enough, but we can't just wait for the end to come. Maybe if we believe strongly enough we have a shot." I hold out my hand. "We have to try."

"Of course you do," says Grandma Pearl, appearing beside me in her own personal bubble.

"Grandma!" I run to her and hold on tight. "But you said this isn't your fight."

Grandma Pearl looks at me. "Obviously I was wrong. It's all our fight, and you now have five! Count me in. I'm a strong half-fairy myself."

"Make that five and a half," says Father, who looks at me. "I'll try my hardest to remember what I've learned." He turns. "Hello, Mother."

"Son." Grandma Pearl beams and grasps his hand.

"We have six!" Trixie cries, rushing to take my other hand. "I believe. I truly believe!"

Will all of us half-fairies make up for the fact that we aren't whole? It *has* to be enough. I will it to be. The group of us form a circle. Jocelyn stands at the outskirts and winds up a fireball.

"We'll hold her off till you get into position," she says as Ollie brandishes his sword.

"Repeat after me," Grandma Pearl instructs. "Power of fairy might, take this wicked witch and drive her from all lands and sight."

"Is that a quorum, I see? How quaint!" Alva says, laughing. "And lead by an old crone like you, Pearl? For the love of Grimm, I didn't even know you were still alive!" Her eyes glint. "No matter. You won't be for long. And this quorum will never work. You aren't full fairies! You don't have enough power in the lot of you."

"Power of fairy might, take this wicked witch and drive her from all lands and sight," we repeat.

Our collective hands start to glow, but it's faint. If only we had more fairies. We need more power. I glance at Anna watching from the sidelines.

"Again!" Grandma Pearl commands.

"Power of fairy might, take this wicked witch and drive

her from all lands and sight." Our hands continue to glow, but Alva is unaffected. Around us, the curse grows closer, sucking in the nearest trees.

Alva raises her wand and aims at our circle. "You aren't powerful enough to stop this curse, Gillian Cobbler! You never have been!" She looks at me. "You are and always will be nothing more than a petty thief. Say goodbye to your precious Enchantasia!"

I keep chanting. Then someone brushes my fingers.

Anna is reaching for my hand.

Time seems to stop as I look at my younger sister. There is so much hurt between us that I don't know what to say. All I know is that we're as different as can be, but that's not a bad thing. Not when she's choosing good. I let go of Father's hand for a split second and take Anna's in my own. Father takes Anna's hand, too, and together they repeat after me.

"Power of fairy might, take this wicked witch and drive her from all lands and sight." Our hands glow again, brighter than before. "Power of fairy might, take this wicked witch and drive her from all lands and sight."

Our hands start to glow orange, and the light emitting

from the egg on the rock starts to dim. It's working! A vortex appears directly behind Alva.

"It can't be!" Alva shouts.

"Power of fairy might, take this wicked witch and drive her from all lands and sight!" we say again, and the vortex spins faster, pulling Alva into it. The light from the egg goes out completely.

"No!" Alva cries, but there is nowhere left for her to turn.

"Power of fairy might, take this wicked witch and drive her from all lands and sight!" We say one last time.

And Alva disappears into thin air.

CHAPTER 17

What Comes Next?

Together we stand in stunned silence, staring at the place Alva reigned only moments before. A ray of light beams down from the red moon and the air is suddenly calm.

Alva is gone.

But at what cost?

That is what I'm thinking as we hold on to one another and stare off into the distance at FTRS, smoking and in pieces. The castle I called home for so long is destroyed. My brothers, Jax, and our beloved teachers are missing or lost to us. Enchantasia still stands, but our victory does not feel as sweet as it should.

Finally, I let go of Anna's hand.

"Gilly?" she starts to say.

But I'm too upset to talk to her. "Don't move." She sits down on a rock, looking lost. Mother, however, runs over, saying nothing as she pulls Anna into her arms. The two of them weep. I walk over to the golden egg on the rock and pick it up, feeling its weight.

Quack!

Peaches waddles up beside me and pecks her beak into my legs. *Quack! Quack! Quack!* Wilson scurries out of a nearby bush, and I stoop down to pick him up as Peaches continues to act frantic. Wilson is squeaking madly too.

"I don't understand what you're saying when you talk that fast!" I tell him as the others gather round. Peaches is flapping her wings wildly. Suddenly she starts to cough. Seconds later, she chokes up a phlegm-covered lamp. This time it's returned to normal size.

"Quick! Someone rub the lamp and see if Darlene is okay!" Maxine says.

"Ooh! I'll do it!" Jocelyn says, her eyes turning almost green with envy.

Ollie swipes it from her. "I wish to see the lady of the lamp," he says, and Darlene oozes out of her home.

As soon as she sees Maxine, she bursts into tears. "We're

still here? Oh my word, I thought we were done for!" Darlene says. "How are you all still here? Why did I have the sudden sensation of being swallowed? And who is my new master?"

"That would be me!" Ollie says, and Grandma Pearl clears her throat. "But, um, I wasn't going to use the wishes, unless you want out of your lamp or you can bring back everyone we just lost." We look at her hopefully.

Darlene's smile fades. "I'm afraid those truly lost in battle cannot be brought back through wishing." My heart plummets. "But I can return the people that Stiltskin's Squad did away with in his second wish—like the teachers of Royal Academy and the princesses. As for those whisked away in battle, let's bring them all back here. Shall we?"

"Darlene!" Maxine cries. "Bring them back! Please!"

"I need a wish," Darlene reminds her and looks at Ollie.

"I wish for our teachers and adult friends to be returned to us from wherever they are in battle or, uh, on vacation!" Ollie says. Darlene closes her eyes, says a few words, there is a gust of wind, and *poof*! Headmistress Flora, Professor Harlow, Madame Cleo—via mirror, Blackbeard, Professor Wolfington, Professor Sebastian, Red, Robin Hood, Beauty, and even AG appear in front of us. Everyone starts cheering while Jocelyn runs for her sister, and AG runs for Kayla and Maxine.

"We'll go check on the other children!" Red declares, hitching a ride on one of Robin's arrows. The two head off into the cornfields to look for more kids and survey the damage.

I am thankful, of course, but my heart still aches in a way it never has before.

"Is everyone all right? Where are Stiltskin and Alva?" Flora asks. "We've been trapped on the other side of the lake. We couldn't get past it since the kingdom was disappearing all around us."

"Mother!" Azalea and Dahlia burst through the trees and into Flora's arms as Angelina and Kayla quickly fill the teachers in on what's happened.

Reunions are happening all over the place. They're just not mine. Mother has a hand on Anna's shoulder and is talking quietly with Father as Trixie picks daisies nearby. Does my younger sister understand what's happened? I can't stop thinking of my brothers.

Harlow puts a hand on my shoulder. "You did good."

"Not good enough," I whisper.

"Our best is always good enough," Professor Sebastian says, coming up beside her. "Unfortunately, when it comes to love and war, we don't always get a happily ever after. I heard about Jax." My eyes well with tears. "And I have something you might want to see."

He pulls a piece of parchment out of his jacket. I see the handwriting and know right away it's Jax's. "He handed it in last night before… Well, I thought you might want to read it."

I take it from him, fighting back tears.

ASSIGNMENT FOR: Professor Sebastian at Fairy Tale Reform School

SENT FROM: Fairy Tale Reform School (while I still can!)

FIVE YEARS FROM NOW I WILL BE…

BY: Prince Jaxon

I know what you're thinking: Five years from now this prince will be part of the royal court.

Well, not so fast.

Look, being prince means I have that right, I guess, but as the kids at Royal Academy have shown, not everyone born royal is meant to rule.

I'd love to explore my options before I decide my place in the kingdom. I'm a good negotiator, a good speaker, and I think I'm a pretty decent guy, so I feel like spending time among the villagers and championing their causes would be a great use of my time. There are so many wonderful organizations out there that could use a boost from a prince's words— and I don't mean that vainly. I just mean if my voice can help promote action for others, why not help where I can?

I have a lot of ideas and much I want to see happen in Enchantasia in the future, so maybe I will wind up on that royal court eventually after all. I guess I'll just need a queen.

And maybe, just maybe, I already have one in mind.

"I didn't get to grade it yet, but I feel like an A would have been fitting," Professor Sebastian says softly.

"I agree," I say, choking back tears. I try not to think about the last sentence of his paper.

"I also have a second wish!" Ollie says, trying to help lighten the mood. "I wish the people of Enchantasia no longer think of us kids as villains."

"Oh, thank the genies, that's a good one!" Darlene agrees and reverses Stiltskin's other wish as well. A shock wave seems to wash over us like the wind, and Darlene smiles. "Done."

Seconds later, we hear a tingling sound. A message is coming across Madame Cleo's mirror.

Kayla reads it out loud. "All safe at royal court. Royal Academy was unharmed, but everyone is a wreck. Is everyone here okay? What's happened? Feels like we were all under Princess Rose's sleeping curse. Will get there as soon as we can to check on the rest of you. Raz."

"Well, that's a relief," Flora says. She eyes the castle and frowns. "We may need their help housing the students till we can get them all home…if their areas of the kingdom are still here. We'll have to send Red and Robin out to see what's left of Enchantasia."

"Home?" Maxine asks. "But FTRS is our home!"

"If you haven't noticed, we don't have a home to go back to," Ollie points out. "It was destroyed in the curse."

"It will take years to rebuild," Professor Wolfington says sadly. "I'm afraid we'll have to find other ways to continue to help the children of Enchantasia change their ways."

"Don't be sad," Beauty tells us. "We can create a pop-up castle or ask Royal Academy to let us run some classes there. There is always a way to continue our work!"

"And hand in homework," Professor Sebastian says, looking at me. "My assignment still stands."

"But Jax…" Kayla starts to say, and everyone grows quiet again.

I turn away so no one can see my tears.

"I wish I could help with the others," Darlene says again. "I so wish that, but I can't do that or rebuild what the curse has taken away, I'm afraid. Wishes don't overrule curses. But you do have one more wish," she reminds Ollie. "So what is it? I'm looking forward to getting back to my lamp and the genie community, even if I will be banished for two weeks for banishing Stiltskin. It was worth it! In fact, if I could make a wish, it would be that you hide me somewhere truly safe so I don't have to grant any more wishes for a good long while."

"You can come stay with me," Grandma Pearl says. "I don't get many visitors."

"You will now." Father pats her hand. "I think we're long overdue for a visit. We all could use a vacation after we find the boys." He swallows hard.

BOOM!

There is a thunderous sound of something descending at alarming speed. We all dive out of the way just in time to see a beanstalk reach the ground and embed itself into the dirt. I look up and see it stretches clear into the cloud.

Erp claps his hands excitedly at the sight of the stalk and tries to climb it.

"Wait!" Jack tells him. "It's coming in reverse. That means someone's coming down."

Whoever they are is so high up, I can't see them. Erp finally gets frustrated and climbs up to greet them. Halfway up, he stops and comes back down with something clutched in his large hand. When he reaches the bottom, he opens his palm.

Jax, Han, and Hamish are nestled inside.

Everyone goes berserk trying to reach them first. Mother and Father are crying, Trixie is screaming, and I'm running for the three of them, laughing through my tears.

"Gilly!" Han's eyes are wide. "We saw Cloud City!"

"And met real giants!" Hamish says. "Jax introduced us to everyone and then said when the coast is clear, we have to head home. We heard the cheers from above and headed back."

"I thought we lost you," I say, looking at Jax but meaning all of them.

"I thought so too." Jax nurses his wounded shoulder, which is now bandaged. "But I guess you can't keep a good trickster down." He grins at me. "Did I worry you again?"

"No. Not at all!" I argue. "You had my brothers. *That's* why I was worried."

"Uh-huh. *That's* why," Ollie says and our friends laugh.

I blush slightly. Jax is probably my closest friend, and that's all there is to it.

For now.

I feel a peck in the back of my legs again. *Quack! Quack! Quack!* Peaches starts again.

"What now?" I huff. "Maxine, will you call your attack duck off?"

Peaches quacks madly at her too.

"What do you mean it didn't fully work the way the curse was meant to and it can be partially reversed?" Maxine asks. She picks up the golden egg. "Uh-huh. Yes," she answers Peaches's quacks. "So Peaches says the reason the curse took so long to work is because it wasn't a full-size golden egg. Yes, a lot of FTRS was destroyed, but the rest of the kingdom is still intact." Everyone cheers. "Peaches said she tried to tell you this earlier when the curse started, but no one would listen."

Peaches glares at me and burps.

That duck...

"Thank you, Peaches," I say, and the duck waddles away.

"Stiltskin's story ended exactly as it should have," Angelina says as she clutches his villain book. "He lost what he most wanted, and good prevails. Thanks to Gilly's strong belief, we fought the darkness and won."

I look at Grandma Pearl. "I tried to believe in myself and remember we're never really alone. As lost as we may feel, we can defeat the darkness together."

"She's right," Father says and puts an arm around his mother. Grandma Pearl's wings flutter.

"All that's left to do is bring back the school—with a few modifications. Remember, I still get another wish," Ollie says, his eyes twinkling.

"Oliver, don't do anything foolish," Headmistress Flora says.

"You bring that lamp back to your place as soon as he's done," I hear Harlow tell my grandmother. "No more wishing for this crew."

"I was just thinking a pirate ship wing, and maybe a new gym," Ollie tells her.

"Oh, and a bigger place for the magical fairy pets to hang out!" Maxine adds.

"A larger potions lab?" Jocelyn suggests.

"And a second wing for daytime students," Professor Sebastian says, and we all look at him. "This crew has clearly graduated—once their papers are turned in—but obviously, continued guidance on a daily basis would be my recommendation."

"Do you have room for new students?" I hear someone ask.

I turn and see Anna standing awkwardly with Mother. Everyone looks at my younger sister. "I know I came here once before and did everything wrong."

"*Everything*," I repeat sharply, folding my arms across my chest.

"And my actions almost brought about the end of Enchantasia as we know it," she adds. "But if anyone needs helps learning how to be reformed, it's me, and the rest of the Stiltskin squad, who are probably hiding out in the woods as we speak." Headmistress Flora is quiet. "I know I don't deserve a second chance, but—"

"Everyone deserves a second chance, child," Professor Sebastian says. "It's what you do with that chance that tells us who you could are—and you, from what we've heard, turned against one of our world's biggest villains."

Anna's eyes are full of tears. "I want to be good like Gilly."

My heart breaks a little. "And I want you to be you. Whoever you are—as long as it's good, of course."

Anna runs over to hug me. I don't let go.

Anna isn't good yet, but she obviously isn't all that bad either. She's a bit like all of us, trying hard to do the right thing and sometimes failing. But that's what Fairy Tale Reform School is for, to help us learn how to get things right and make the kingdom a better place.

"Then let's get this school back so we can start working again, shall we?" Flora asks.

"With pleasure." Grandma Pearl taps the golden egg.

"What was undone, please be redone—as much as you can!"

We watch in reverent awe as our school glistens and glows in front of our eyes, reshaping, regrowing into our school. It's not the same, of course, and there are still things that will have to be rebuilt and grown, but we take off at a run toward it anyway. In the distance, I see Robin Hood and Red zipping across arrows and depositing children at the school's new gates. Ollie has obviously made his last wish too. There's a pirate ship on top of the boys' dorm and what appears to be an entire zoo area for the Magical Fairy Pets. There's even a sign for a village simulation shop where students can "try being good" in a controlled environment.

"Want to go check it out?" I ask Anna, holding out my hand.

Anna looks at her new school in wonder and smiles as she puts her hand in mine. "Yes."

"Come on, thief!" Jax calls, running ahead of me.

My sister and I take off at a run, as fast as our legs will take us into the fiery-red moonlight.

Assignment for: Professor Sebastian at Fairy Tale Reform School

Sent from: 5 Boot Way (My new home address! Our house has been rebuilt!)

Five Years from Now I Will Be...

By: Gillian Cobbler

It feels strange thinking about five years from now when I've already lived a lifetime at Fairy Tale Reform School. Let's face it: I've done a lot. How many twelve-year-olds do you know who have faced down two major villains, visited Cloud City, and fought a dragon, a wyvern, and a possessed princess—and lived to tell about it?

What do I really want to happen in five years? I want to see the kingdom at peace.

I'm sure that's not possible. But if I wind up working at the Dwarf Police Squad like I envision, I'll be there with a shiny badge, ready to take down any villains or delinquents who need to learn how to be good. But maybe I should be thinking bigger.

Why stop at just helping the kids of Enchantasia Village when I could be doing more for the kingdom as a whole? Maybe I'm meant to help run this place. Hey, it could happen. If the Royal Academy kids can rebel at what it means to be a prince or a princess, why can't I buck the whole system and run Enchantasia as a commoner? I've seen a lot and have a lot of ideas about how to make this place great. I know how to work well as part of a team now. Plus, I know a great group of kids who would make the coolest, most well-rounded court around.

GRADE: B+! Impressive dreams, Gilly. I wouldn't be surprised if this actually happens! See you at class this Monday, where we'll discuss what it means to be in charge of a kingdom. Keep up the good work. —Professor S

Acknowledgments

As a child, I always struggled watching *Cinderella*. While my friends cheered for Cinderella's happy ending, I worried about the Wicked Stepmother. Would she go to fairy-tale jail for what she'd done to Cinderella? Who would watch over the stepsisters if she did go to jail? Left to their own devices, would they, too, become villains someday?

I wanted the Wicked Stepmother to have her own chance to tell her story, and I thought about her journey for years before I tried to rewrite the villain stories we know. Giving them a chance to teach other children on the path to wickedness how to be good, in a story told through the eyes of a plucky pickpocket who must learn to think of more than just herself, has been one of the most rewarding experiences I've ever had.

I am indebted to three editors who helped me tell these tales the last few years: Aubrey Poole, who read the proposal for *Flunked* and immediately wanted to tell Gilly's story with me; Kate Prosswimmer, who became a wonderful collaborator as the world of FTRS continued to grow; and Molly Cusick, who came in at the end to champion the series and help me get it across the finish line.

I can't think of a better home for this series than Sourcebooks. They've been incredible at shouting about the series from rooftops. I am forever indebted to Dominique Raccah, Steve Geck, Heather Moore, Lizzie Lewandowski, Stefani Sloma, Margaret Coffee, and Cassie Gutman, and to Nicole Hower and Mike Heath, whose gorgeous covers have led to countless discussions at school assemblies.

I also couldn't have done it without my agent, Dan Mandel, who has taken such good care of this series, and Laura Dail, who first found the series a home.

And finally, to all of you teachers, librarians, and readers who have reached out to me over the last few years to talk about Fairy Tale Reform School or tell me how these books changed you, thank you for taking a chance on me and a feisty young girl who wanted to change the fairy-tale world. I'm forever grateful that I've gotten to take this journey with you.

WELCOME TO ROYAL ACADEMY!

From the desk of the Fairy Godmother*

Headmistress Olivina would like to cordially welcome* you to Royal Academy for your first year of ruler training!

Please arrive with a training wand, a mini magical scroll, several quills, and no fewer than three pairs of dress shoes. (Please note: glass slippers should have scuffed soles to prevent injuries due to heavily waxed floors.)

Personal stylists and tailors will be on-site to assist all students in creating their signature royal style. We look forward to seeing you one week from today!

*The word welcome *is only a formality! Attendance at RA is mandatory for all young royals in the kingdom. Questions should be sent by magical scroll to the Fairy Godmother's office.*

JEN CALONITA'S
BRAND-NEW SERIES

BOOK 2

BOOK 1

NOT EVERYONE BORN ROYAL
IS MEANT TO RULE

Scan the code or turn the page for a sneak peek of Misfits.

ONCE THERE WAS A GIRL...

H old still. I just want to help you." I keep my voice calm yet firm. If she moves too quickly, she could do more damage. I need to be careful not to spook her.

"That's a good girl," I coo, taking a step closer. "Stay right where you are. You're safe now."

Crack! My bare foot snaps a twig, startling her. She hobbles farther into the brush, making it hard for me to see anything but her panicked eyes. If she moves any deeper into the branches, I won't be able to reach her.

"It's okay," I tell her as some of our friends quietly gather around to watch me work.

I step deeper into the thicket, the chittering of the insects intensifying in the shady trees that surround me. The air is hot, and I'm sweating despite having left my jacket and skirt back in the clearing. I snag a vine from above me and use it to tie back my pale-blond locks. She's watching with interest as I fix my hair.

"I'm not going to hurt you," I promise, my voice barely more than a whisper. Slowly, I pull something from my pocket I know she'll like. I place the handful of cashews I swiped from last night's dinner on a branch between us. She eyes the nuts for a moment, then quickly eats one. Nice!

As she crunches on the nuts, I stay very still, listening for any sounds. I hear an owl hoot in the distance and water babbling in a nearby brook, but for the most part, the forest is unusually quiet.

"Good snack, right?" I ask, trying to make her feel at ease. "I know I look young, but I have a lot of experience doing what I'm doing, so don't be nervous."

She tilts her head at me.

"It's true! Just last week, Nox came to see me for a sore throat, and I mixed him a tonic that cleared it right up. And when Peter lost his sense of smell after having a bad cold, I made a broth that fixed everything." I inch closer to the tangle of brambles where she's perched. She doesn't move, so

I keep talking. "And when Deirdre sprained her ankle after running from a bear in the Hollow Woods, I made her a splint, and now she's walking just fine."

I hold out my hand. She doesn't recoil, but she doesn't move any closer either. Time to bring out the big guns. I strain my neck toward my friends below me. "Deirdre? Can you please back me up here?"

Deirdre takes a flying leap, landing on the tree branch next to me.

Did I mention she's a flying squirrel?

Or that the "she" I'm trying to help is a songbird?

Lily, my bearded dragon, pokes her head out of my shirt pocket to listen to Deirdre's mix of clicks, clucks, and high-pitched squeaks that will hopefully get through to the little red bird with the injured wing. I can only make out parts of what she's saying.

I'm not fluent in squirrel yet.

Not like other humans! Really cares… Knows medicine! She can help… Trust her. We do! Friend!

I smile at that last word. I don't have many friends. When you tell the kids in the schoolyard you can talk to animals, most call you a liar. Or a freak. Some even say you're evil.

Hey, I get it. It's an unusual, uh, *talent* to have, but it's a big part of who I am. Besides, I am really good at this "helping animals" thing.

I notice her wing is sagging. She might have snagged it taking off from a tree, or maybe she bumped into a giant. My animal friends say it happens a lot. The songbird curiously sniffs my fingers with her beak.

"That's it now. Climb in," I say in a soft voice. Deirdre chimes in too, squeaking her encouragement.

Finally, after a moment of hesitation, the bird steps into my steady palm! Below, I hear the chattering cheer of my friends.

"What's your name?" I ask the little bird as I carefully cradle her fragile body.

She chirps in a small singsong voice.

"Scarlet? How lovely to meet you, Scarlet." I stand up and walk her over to my office.

My office is really just a quilt I stole from the maid's quarters. (Mother wanted it tossed anyway.) On the blanket, I have my satchel of herbs that I pinched from the kitchen and mending tools I've gathered from our sewing kits. I store everything in a hollow log near the clearing so no one questions what I'm up to when I go on my "daily walks" beyond our garden gates.

I rinse my hands with the little jug of water I've brought with me, then open my satchel and pull out the small fabric slings I've been making while Mother thought I was practicing my needlepoint. Finding one that looks to be the right size, I get to work, setting the bird's wing as best I can. Scarlet tweets excitedly when I'm finished. Then I mix basil, chamomile, and willow bark seeds together with the water.

"This should help with the pain," I tell her. "Come see me again in a few days, and we'll see how your wing is mending. If you want, we can help you find a safe place to sleep in the meantime." I place the mixture in a tiny thimble and encourage Scarlet to drink. After a few sips, she tweets at me excitedly, and I know she's saying "thank you." She has a sibling that lives in a hollowed-out old oak three trees over so she'll be safe there while she heals. That's a relief.

Everyone is so excited about Scarlet's new sling that they can't keep quiet. Between the neighs, snorts, and chittering from other animals, I'm worried a big, bad wolf—or worse, the main house—will wonder what's going on.

"Keep it down!" I say with a laugh. "You're going to give

us away!" The noise decreases slightly, and I lean back and soak in the sunlight filtering through the trees.

I live for moments like this. Being a creature caretaker is all I've wanted to be. Mother thought it was a phase I'd grow out of, which is why she didn't pay Father any mind when he bought me a leather satchel filled with "animal doctor" supplies. But ever since, I've been pulling spiders out of drinking jugs, mending birds' wings on my bedroom windowsill, rescuing wayward kittens from hungry foxes, and getting an occasional visit from a unicorn that has lost its sense of direction.

I won't be *growing out of it* anytime soon. I don't know how I'm able to talk to animals or know what they need, but I'm smart enough to know you don't give up a gift like that. I hope that someday even creatures beyond Cobblestone Creek will seek me out for help. But first, I need to find someone to teach me proper creature care techniques.

"*Devinaria!*"

I sit up straight. The birds stop chirping. Lily pokes her head out of my pocket again, and we stare at each other worriedly. No one should be looking for me out here. Not when I swore I was going to Mother Hubbard's Tea Shoppe with some girls from class.

"Devinaria! Where are you?"

Drooping dragons! The voice grows louder, and I hear trumpets sounding in the distance. It's as if a royal procession is about to roll right through the forest. I hear footsteps, then heavy breathing, as if someone's running in our direction.

I jump up, trying to put all my supplies away before someone sees them. Then I remember what I'm wearing. I look down at my undergarments and torn shirt and spin around in a desperate search for my skirt. The shirt and bloomers I'm wearing aren't much different from the outfits the boys in the village wear, but the ensemble is definitely not—as my mother would say—"princess appropriate."

"Princess Devinaria!" Our footman Jacques sounds out of breath as he stumbles into the clearing. "There you are!"

I cringe. I *hate* when people call me that. "Devin is just fine, Jacques." I try to maintain an air of dignity as I grab my skirt from a bush and quickly wrap it around my waist, pinning it on the side where I've cut it for easy on-and-off situations. With a ribbon tied and draped down the side, no one can tell I sliced the skirt open (other than Jacques, who has just seen my little trick and looks quite alarmed).

"How, um, did you even find me out here?" I run a hand through my hair and pull out a leaf. "Did you need something?" I ask him.

"Miss, it's urgent!" Jacques's eyes widen as the trumpets sound closer. "Your mother...father...the trumpets... Miss, *it's* coming, and..."

I inhale sharply and stumble backward. Lily flicks her tongue wildly. "No," I whisper.

"Yes!" Jacques insists, grabbing my hand. "Your invitation is here!"

ROYAL ACADEMY

From the desk of the Fairy Godmother

Headmistress Olivina would like to cordially welcome*

Devinaria Nile
of Cobblestone Creek, Enchantasia

to Royal Academy for her first year of princess training!

Please arrive with a training wand, mini magical scroll, several quills, and no fewer than three ball gowns, two petticoats, and three pairs of dress shoes. (Please note: Glass slippers should have scuffed soles to prevent injuries due to heavily waxed floors.)

Personal stylists and tailors will be on-site to assist all students in creating their signature royal style. We look forward to seeing you one week from today!

◇◇◇◇◇◇◇◇

The word welcome *is only a formality! Attendance at RA is <u>mandatory</u> for all young royals in the kingdom. Questions should be sent by magical scroll to the Fairy Godmother's office.*

You Are Cordially Invited

Jacques pulls me through the clearing, and I let him because I'm numb, numb, numb. I've been dreading this day for a long time. My heart pumps harder as we near the grounds of the cottage.

Okay, it's not really a cottage. I just call it that. It's a castle. The word *castle* just sounds so obnoxious. Like, "Sorry I'm late. It's a long coach ride from my castle." I hate when some of the kids at school say things like that. I hear the village kids talking about us sometimes. *Fancy-schmancies* they call our type. If only they could see what I'm wearing right now.

Mother is already pacing at the garden gate as we approach, and that's when I realize I have a bigger problem than the invitation to end all invitations. Such as the fact that my clothes are torn and I'm covered in dirt and leaves when I said I was going to Mother Hubbard's. I dig in my heels on the grass, and Jacques falters.

"Princess!" He strains to keep me moving. "We must… go… Wow, you're strong."

Hanging from tree branches all day is great for upper-body strength.

"I can't go, Jacques." I pull back. "I'm sorry."

"Your mother is waiting!"

"I can't let her see me like this!"

He pulls.

I yank his arm back. We could play tug-of-war all day.

"Devinaria?"

We both turn to the garden gate, where Mother is peering through the ivy that clings to the fence. She has an elaborate updo for a Tuesday afternoon and is even wearing her tiara. Seeing her makes my stomach start doing cartwheels.

I wave. "Hello, Mother."

She steps through the gate with a look of horror on her face. "You? You! *You!*" She's pointing and stuttering as she takes in my appearance. She touches my torn skirt and cries out. Jacques lets go of my arm and slowly steps away from me. He can sense a teakettle about to whistle when he sees one.

"You look lovely today, Mother! How was your luncheon with the royal court?" I curtsy clumsily.

"I left early when I heard what was happening. Get in the house this instant!" She grabs my arm and starts walking. "If we're lucky, we can clean your face and hands before they get here. They're already one château away!"

"How do you know they're coming here?" I ask as Mother pulls me through the garden gate where my lady-in-waiting, Anastasia, is…well…waiting. Her eyes widen as she takes in my disheveled appearance.

"The dove delivered the preliminary invitation to our doorstep an hour ago so you could be ready." Mother pulls a scroll out of her pocket and hands it to me. "And you're clearly *not* ready."

As I skim the scroll, I get a sinking feeling in my chest. "They need me there next week?" Now my voice is shrill. "That's not enough time! I…have nothing to wear." There's no greater travesty in Mother's life than not having the right gown, even for something as informal as a trip to the village.

She waves her hand around. "Of course you have things to wear! Darling, I've been packing your trunk for Royal Academy all year!"

I should have known. "But my hair and my nails... They're a mess!" I falter.

"Done and done!" Mother ticks off each concern with a joyous laugh. "I have maids inside now waiting to help. Devinaria, the *Enchantasia Insider* gives us hints on the week invites will go out, so I'm prepared." She pulls a twig out of my hair with a frown. "I'm sure they can do *something* with this bird's nest of yours."

My heart is pounding faster. It feels as though the garden walls are closing in. I pull away. "But I don't want to go to Royal Academy."

Mother's jaw begins to quiver. "That's nonsense! We've talked about this path for you since you were a toddler. This is your chance to move up the royal ladder! There hasn't been a widespread plague or dragon outbreak in years, so we both know being twelfth in line for the throne will get you nowhere. With any luck and perhaps some fairy magic, you'll meet a prince at Royal Academy so you can rule a small province or kingdom."

"Mother!" I sputter. I can see some of my forest friends peeking through the garden gate. "You'd want a whole village to be wiped out just so I could be queen?"

My voice is louder than I intended, and I realize all the servants are looking at us. Mother's face is crimson. She smiles brightly at them all, then turns back to me. "Don't be ridiculous, Devin. I was just pointing out how difficult your prospects are! What I'm trying to say is that going to RA will give you the best chance of becoming a queen."

"Who says I even want to be a queen?" I counter. "Maybe I'm meant to do something else with my life. Look at all the good work I've been able to do for the creatures of Cobblestone Creek." I motion to the fence. "I know you don't want to admit it, but I have a connection with animals. I can understand them and help them."

Mother turns me away from the servants. "Would you stop saying that?" she whispers. "You sound deranged! It's your destiny to become a ruler!"

"Ah, I see you found Devin." Father walks up behind us. He's dressed in his finest threads, a sash across his chest showcasing the many gold medals he's earned as a commander in Enchantasia's Royal Infantry. He kisses my cheek even though it's sweaty. "Ready for your invitation?" he asks me, but before I can answer, Mother cuts in again.

"Not exactly. She's still going on about her love of animals! We've put up with this childish hobby long enough."

Father puts a hand on her shoulder and says, "Belinda, you can't deny she has a gift."

"Gift? It's a *hobby*." Mother looks at the two of us as if we're conspiring against her. "You must stop encouraging her!" she says to Father, then turns to me. "This is not your future, Devinaria. Royal Academy is! Just look at your cousin, Penelope Claudine. She went to Royal Academy, and now she's married to a king with three castles!"

"I don't want three castles!" I protest. "I don't even need the one castle we have. It's too big."

"Oh, Devin, you're so charming." Mother takes my hand in her free one. She is smiling so earnestly that for a moment I feel bad about how hard I'm fighting her. "What is this really about? Are you nervous about going away to school? Because I am sure you're going to love it there. Royal Academy was created just a few years after your father and I were married, so I never got to go, but it sounds like a dream! Can you imagine having a royal tailor on hand to make you any ball gown you want?"

"But I don't want…" Never mind. I pull my hand away and fold my arms across my chest, ready to restate my case. I hear horses galloping in the distance. The trumpet sound is growing near. I don't have much time.

"Fight me all you like," Mother finally says. "Let your official royalty profile portrait be one of you looking like this! The truth is, you don't have a choice concerning whether you attend or not." She points to the fine print on the bottom of the scroll and makes sure Father sees it too. "All royals of your age must attend RA. It says so right here."

I bite my lip so hard I taste blood. The trumpets are growing louder. Suddenly, the servants open the back doors, and I see men wearing wigs and gold-trimmed white jackets. They're carrying my official proclamation as they march into our garden. There's also a painter with them who immediately begins to sketch my image.

"Her royal portrait!" Mother cries.

She wipes my face and tries to tame my hair, but my eyes are on Father. He's my one hope for avoiding a future that involves Royal Academy. "Father?" I say questioningly. "*Please.*"

I watch his expression closely. It wavers between sadness

and an emotion I can't identify. He places his hands on my shoulders as Mother tries to fluff my skirt. I watch her pull the ribbon out of her own hair and tie it around mine.

"Devin, I tried. I really did," Father says. "But she wouldn't budge on the matter. Even after I explained your extraordinary gift. If anything, it only made her want you more."

She? "You mean Mother?" I question.

Father shakes his head as more guards arrive. If they're surprised by my appearance, they don't say.

"Olivina," Father explains in a whisper. "Royal Academy's headmistress." His eyes search mine. "She says she can see the future, and you, my child, are destined for great things."

ROYAL ACADEMY

Student Supply List for Young Ladies

◇◇◇◇◇◇

If you don't have these books at home—and I expect many of you are well-versed in these teachings already!—please purchase and bring to the first day of orientation. I look forward to many fruitful discussions this school year.

—Headmistress Olivina

Reading List

¤ *Royal Academy Rules* by Fairy Godmother Olivina

¤ *Beyond the Glass Slipper: How to Nab a Prince without the Right Shoes* by Cinderella

¤ *Cursed Childhood: How to Avoid Being a Target for Sleeping Curses and Poison Apples* by Fairy Godmother Olivina, foreword by Princess Rose

¤ *Rescue Plans and Other Things a Princess Should Never Leave Her Castle Without* by Fairy Godmother Olivina

¤ *Ten Ways to a Happier Imprisonment* by Rapunzel

¤ *Mirror Image: Finding the Royal Within* by Snow White

Optional Reading

¤ *From Rags to Royals: 1,001 Beauty Tips from Princesses* compiled by Marta Marigold, RA's Official Beautification Expert

About the Author

Jen Calonita has interviewed everyone from Reese Witherspoon to Justin Timberlake, but the only person she's ever wanted to trade places with is Disney's Cinderella. When Jen isn't plotting, she's working on stories in the Royal Academy Rebels series. She lives in Merrick, New York, with her husband, two sons, and their Chihuahuas. Visit Jen at jencalonitaonline.com.